IN
OTHER
WORDS

WORDS

OTHER

IN

IN OTHER WORDS

Edited by
Mainspring Arts

**Eight Stories,
Eight Unheard
Voices**

unbound

First published in 2021

Unbound
Level 1, Devonshire House, One Mayfair Place, London W1J 8AJ
www.unbound.com
All rights reserved

Text design by PDQ Digital Media Solutions Ltd

A CIP record for this book is available from the British Library

ISBN 978-1-80018-032-1 (hardback)
ISBN 978-1-80018-033-8 (paperback)
ISBN 978-1-80018-034-5 (ebook)

Printed in Great Britain by Clays Ltd, Elcograf S.p.A

1 3 5 7 9 8 6 4 2

*For everyone who has to shout a little
louder to have their voices heard*

In Other Words is the result of Square Peg Stories, a creative writing scheme aimed specifically at autistic writers that Mainspring Arts ran in London between November 2016 and May 2017. Eight participants were selected to take part in a series of workshops and mentoring sessions led by published authors, with the aim of each writer producing an original short story. Workshop leaders included author and poet Joanne Limburg and YA fantasy author Corinne Duyvis, who are both autistic. The workshops were designed to meet the specific needs of the participants, meaning the writers were able to relax into their environment and develop their talent.

Mainspring Arts is an innovative charity dedicated to increasing neurodiversity in the arts. We do this by facilitating workshops and artist development opportunities, providing free resources and creating platforms for neurodivergent artists to present work. We believe that neurodivergent people should have the opportunity to represent their own voices and experiences, and we exist to help them do it. Other projects include Springboard, a regular scratch night for neurodivergent performers; Square Peg Scripts, a playwriting opportunity; and Two Metres ApART, a digital museum of work by neurodivergent artists.

CONTENTS

FOREWORD

I'm honoured to have been asked to write this foreword for *In Other Words*, a collection of eight stories by eight authors, curated by Mainspring Arts. The narratives are as varied in subject and style as the stories are lively and imaginative. 'A Conversation of Sparrows' by Jon Adams begins the anthology with an intriguing mystery set in a recent garden and a wartime past, shadowed by psychiatric damage. Clues to what is going on are revealed with a mature, unhurried pace, and the story rewards a second reading. There is also more to the world of Damian Sawyer's 'Standard Candles' than meets the eye, where a single mother is helped at the darkest point of her young life by an angelic figure. Hope is shown to be as indestructible and ever-present in dark places as stars. Stars also feature in Wiskey's 'Light Revolution', a quirky, pun-loving, science-fiction-slash-comedy-of-academic-manners-slash-utopian vision of the future, following a shift in the nature of light and the appearance of an eighth colour in the visible spectrum. It's tempting to see a metaphor for neuro-atypicality in this eighth colour. Next is 'The Crows' by Kate Roy, an occult fantasy in the tradition of H. P. Lovecraft, whose protagonist finds himself alone and trapped in a university. Laws of physics have been bent out of shape, and the use of imagery is especially memorable. 'The Last Tree' by Sarah is narrated by the last tree in the world. I admired how this ecological fable about humanity's mistreatment of the natural world mirrors (and is mirrored in) the story of a boy who befriends the sentient tree, their relationship striking a strong emotional chord. Esther Lowery's compelling story 'The Clockmaker' takes the reader back in time to Victorian London, where a likeable, poor young woman struggles to survive in a hostile world and builds a temporary bridge across the social divide. Luke Matthews' story 'The Beach House' starts off pretty dark and gets slowly darker. The author exhibits a strong sense of voice and plot as Nick, his narrator, constructs his own private hell. *In Other Words* ends on a light-hearted note with Richard Baskett's 'Winona the Angelic Wizard', a magic caper especially rich in talking animals.

Writing, finishing, editing and polishing a story is no mean feat, and congratulations are due to all the authors in this volume. As someone with a personal interest in autism, I began the collection with my antennae alert for signs of the authors' first-hand knowledge of autism. The use of 'split-screen' narratives or the non-mainstream viewpoints in the stories could be attributable to neuro-atypicality, but these could be traced just as plausibly to fertile imaginations and an authorial judgement that this structure or that point of view is the best method to tell the story. Perhaps this blurry border between the imagination, creative writing and autism is the point of the collection. The imagination is not a neurotypical place, whether its host brain is neurotypical or not. We all have stories to tell, whether we are neurotypical or not. We all share a human urge to tell stories, neurotypical or not. We all share an appetite to read and hear stories, neurotypical or not. The authors, the editors and I hope the reader will find much to enjoy in the following stories. Neurotypical or not.

David Mitchell, 2020

INTRODUCTION

Let's say I presented you with two words – 'autism' and 'fiction' – and asked you what came to mind. Most probably you would mention *The Curious Incident of the Dog in the Night-Time*; a few of you might recall another novel, *The Rosie Project*, or TV dramas like *The Bridge* or *The 'A' Word*. These are all works of fiction, and they all feature central characters who are described as autistic. They are *about* autistic people, in other words, but, like the vast majority of texts with autism as their subject, they are not written by us.

In recent years, autistic people have begun to address this gap in our representation. We have started to write about ourselves, and about the world as we experience it. There are tweets, blogs, newspaper and magazine articles, poems and a growing number of books – 'autiebiographies', as they are sometimes called. But if you have come across any of the fictional autistic characters I've mentioned, you might expect this, since fictional autistic characters, among other things, are identified as such by their habit of blurting out the truth in great detail. And what's autobiography if it isn't that?

One possible answer is that autobiography is a narrative version of the self, constructed out of a complex negotiation between lived experience and the conventions of medium and genre. In other words, it's rarely as naïve a form of writing as it first appears, and, by extension, autobiographers are not necessarily naïve writers. 'Autiebiographers' are not necessarily naïve either. They employ their knowledge of craft as any other writer would. They construct things: sentences, paragraphs, scenes, stories.

All the writers – the autistic writers – whose work is presented in this anthology have chosen to deploy these craft elements to write fiction. Taken all together, their short stories show just how broad a category this can be. Luke Matthews' 'The Beach House', Jon Adams' 'A Conversation of Sparrows' and Damian Sawyer's 'Standard Candles' employ social realism and invite us to empathise with their central characters as they go through traumatic experiences. All three shift back and forth in time, with Adams and Sawyer also moving between the viewpoints of different characters, and between different points in human history. Esther Lowery's 'The Clockmaker', meanwhile, is set entirely in the Victorian era, and is a thoroughly satisfying piece of historical fiction.

'Standard Candles' also possesses supernatural elements, linking it with a second group of stories which take place in imagined worlds. In Kate Roy's 'The Crows', we follow her protagonist on an unsettling, sometimes terrifying journey through alternative dimensions. Wiskey's 'Light Revolution' imagines the dawning of a new, messianic age, heralded by a piece of toilet graffiti, which is discovered by a scientist struggling to come to terms with her somewhat unusual marriage. In 'The Last Tree', Sarah takes the reader to a bleak future, poignantly observed by its non-human narrator. Richard Baskett also extends this imaginative sympathy for the non-human in 'Winona the Angelic Wizard', a fairy story for grown-ups which features a cast of eccentric talking animals.

As a tutor on the Square Peg Stories writing course, I was privileged to work with the writers of these stories, and to witness the work developing from initial ideas, through successive drafts, to the finished versions in this anthology. I've found so much to appreciate, admire and enjoy in them. So will you.

Joanne Limburg, October 2020

A CONVERSATION OF SPARROWS
(*EINE KONVERSATION VON SPATZEN*)

JON ADAMS

The garden was empty. They had watched as she slept untouched for four years seemingly unloved by anyone other than themselves. They had watched as plants, left unkempt, grew wild, invading those spaces they had never been intended for but had since settled in perfectly. They waited for someone, anyone, to unlock the back door and enter the garden along the narrow weed-strewn side path, longing for someone to look around, to care for them all again. They'd grown accustomed to the door being opened only when the Gardener or his wife attended to the rubbish or used the washing line. But these two never entered for pleasure, or so it seemed. Life, they felt, the heart of a garden, a celebration of growing, the core of her very soul was long fledged and flown. Then one morning, they observed a change. The Gardener had filled a new green bird feeder and hung it up on the frayed washing line. Rising above the chatter on the rooftop and gutter, they all watched and waited. It took three weeks until they summoned up the courage to return after this non-routine intervention. But when they did, they brought with them a song. A song of renewed conversation.

1

Four years before this, the Gardener had sat in the bath for three days, slumped, knees upwards, the water lapping at his chin. It wasn't actually three whole days as he'd taken accidental tea breaks when the phone rang and had slept in a bed. But it was close. By choice, he now lived gentle cycles of release as the water cooled, followed by a foot-spun refresh of hot water when he noticed he was shivering. Always having loved water, even now at fifty-five he'd retained a childlike delight, relishing the touch on his skin as he slipped in. Memories flooded through him. One especially, of swimming in the dark aged eleven. He'd learnt to do this in Devon with the green glow of plankton enclosing him, pulsing with each hand-stroke or foot-kick. The Gardener especially enjoyed remembering those beaches where sand-surfed hymns were sung for wave-makers lost in mutual embrace, but these weren't the reasons for this ongoing marathon. He was searching for an answer. It had started as a plain bath, the sort you'd take after a long day in the garden, a *soak your bones* bath, not a *wash for the day* bath. He was frightened. He couldn't say why, and couldn't get out of the bath – or rather didn't want to leave the cocoon of warmth he had spun. His fear was not all irrational, not measured either, but was there each day, its fingers closed firmly round his chest holding tight. Today was bad. Not only had he woken as usual at 4:23 a.m. in a cold, sticky sweat but the nightmares had strayed into his daylight. He could taste the difference, the progress of degeneration as the days clicked past each other and he fell in slow motion. Closing his eyes, he deliberately let himself become distracted, lost in the warmth, becalmed, soothed, every neuron reciting in unison a new self-wrapped prayer for these waters to cleanse him, pardon him and take away his sin.

The Gardener had become unwell and in the May after his mother's passing, he was diagnosed with Post Traumatic Stress Disorder. He'd acquired this from an accident that he was either reluctant or unable to talk about. Not long after this accident, the dreams had begun, often waking him in a cold sweat early in the morning. They weren't dreams you'd call *horrific*. They were more subtly dangerous, escaping collapsing buildings or being left alone away from home without any means of returning. He'd also started to drink to hide the unidentifiable fears that were now becoming frequent visitors during the day. Soon he had become reclusive. He was all flight and no fight, unable to leave the house or care for the garden. He felt so frightened at times but he didn't know of what: each day, the dread of something unknown he *knew* was coming. These fears burned like desires from the inside out, consuming all, leaving him physically shattered. He felt he was drowning, as if each day he was undertaking a forced midnight summer swim wearing a winter coat with pebble-filled pockets. Asleep, he felt he was walking on top of a cathedral roof, arms outstretched, balancing in the wind with only a few feet until he ran out of space and fell.

He knew he needed to learn more on that day in May when he found out an unwelcome revolting, revolving sun was growing within him. To occupy himself, to give a purpose to a faltering existence, he started reading and subsequently remembering. The more he read, researching trauma, the closer he came to reconciling his future challenges. He remembered as a child his uncle had pressed a medal into his hand whilst closing his own fingers about his, saying, 'From a dead soldier in Italy,' and then nothing else. Then after his uncle died, he had realised by keeping these few simple words safe, he'd taken upon himself the acts of remembrance for both of these men. His grandfather never spoke about the war either. He'd asked him a question once and been hushed by his grandmother before he could ever understand why his grandad sat there silent, eyes distant yet wide open, seemingly elsewhere. His mother had shared family rumours of gas attacks and being buried by shelling, and as the Gardener's condition progressively worsened, he learned there were worlds locked inside and understood that need for silence. Whilst at a Sunday military fair, he picked up a photograph of a young soldier with a horse and wondered who he was; what was his story? He imagined him and others, on all sides, those who had seen or done things beyond their choice and the suffering that followed. When he got home, he broke down in tears, not for himself but because he wanted to hold his grandfather and tell him he now understood.

The Soldier remembered the rockets. Sitting back tight against the dirty wall, tired of the shelling, shaking, he longed for the taste and the touch of the farm and the sight of those rockets. These weren't childlike toys or fireworks he was picturing; these were real rockets released during one long hot summer fifteen years earlier. He could see their silent white trails appearing as if by magic, reaching up into the blueness, often drifting overhead minutes later as the breezes intervened. He'd always stop to watch, often caught by surprise out in the fields, but when he could, when he knew, he'd climb the tree, high on the edge of their land: this was now his oaken grandstand. One day, he watched, his hand firm against his forehead, as one arched low overhead, coming to earth in the field near the tree, starting a small fire. He was the first there, furiously beating out the flames with his jacket just ahead of a small car full of men, attracted by his waving, who shouted excitedly as they joined in the stamping before retrieving the now blackened silver tube. One turned and thanked him, handing him a piece of broken fin. These were real scientists, he eagerly told his mother as he opened his hand to reveal diamonds of shining aluminium, adding he was determined to be a real scientist one day too. She smiled. She always smiled, even as she was washing, even as she sat and repaired his scorched jacket, the only casualty of the day.

The beautiful sharpened pencils remained still and impotent on the Gardener's dining table. Not even his wife dared to touch them, although she longed to do so. His words were locked intimately within the carbon; unwritten, unseen, an unspoken secret whispered to no one. His story had unfolded, time passing through but unformed by presence of hand or voice. The Gardener had felt unable to talk for so long. He'd felt that their sharing, if he could have done so, would have robbed him of comfort, forced a confrontation with a real world where everything eventually passed away, spoilt by misunderstanding and self-encouraged decay. It was the same with the garden: it had been nurtured with glee from bare brick and glass a few years before. Wild impenetrable thorn cut away to reveal lives that had become smothered, overshadowed, overtaken by others. These souls he cared for, these he gave a voice, a chance of fulfilment. But he'd reluctantly abandoned them when the empathy he'd been able to control far outgrew any capacity to cope.

The Soldier loved nature, often lying in the fields drawing the patterns of the stars and their geometry. He collected interesting stones the plough unearthed and, familiar with the seasons and the wildlife they brought with them, he watched the birds in particular. As a child, he frequently dreamed of moon men, monsters and space travel, reading stories of the scientific possibilities to come. He smiled recalling how, earlier, in that 'summer of rockets,' he'd read a story from the United States about the discovery of a new planet. They had named this one Pluto, the ninth furthest from the sun. He had tried to imagine those vast stretches of space by pacing across a

field leaving a trail of stones but became skilful only at
estimating distance, which served him well. What had
given him hope during that summer was both Pluto's
discoverer and the fact that this 'rocket man' lived on a
farm, so anything was possible, it seemed, maybe even for
him. Still shaking, still smiling, he closed his eyes against
the noise and soon he slept fitfully. His dreams were of
sparrows, his dreams were of being a million miles away.

In the Gardener's mind, the briar patches thickened.
This *fear forest* that others had seeded with word and
deed against his will was now grown, blocking both sun
and moon. Each night in his sleep he was compelled
to walk between these malevolent trees, barefoot,
vulnerable, and again without rest or sustenance during
daylight. He knew he had to act, he had to cut this forest
down and, after pulling splinters and binding his feet,
this he did with tools forged of steel and the feathers of
birds.

That morning, the Gardener awoke from the dark
with the light still on. For the first few seconds, there
was a hope, a remembrance, as the dreams untangled
themselves before letting the previous day's heat
intrude. He didn't or couldn't move, lying completely
still, the covers pulled over the child inside him that
was struggling to cope. He hadn't slept for long. Today,
he promised himself, would be different. The ginger
cat had sat in the small of the Gardener's back all night
and stirred in parallel with any movement he may
have unconsciously made. The rhythm of the animal's

imperative cleaning comforted him as he started to count, only to feel the cat leave before he reached double figures – but it was just to sit on his chest instead, looking him in the eye whilst whispering 'a food call to action'. The Gardener lived with his wife but they rarely slept in the same room since his accident, as did the cat. He was always awake early and she needed her sleep. She was slightly younger and had always encouraged him the best she could but those PTSD days and nights were dark and long, which had made her weary.

He wasn't cold leaving the bed covers, unmade, rumpled into micro-mountains, the light switched off, an early curtain glow, bathroom water's singing extinguished by fingers turning the now warm tap. He carefully negotiated the stairs as the ginger cat pushed past beneath his feet and across the magenta carpet. He opened the kitchen door that the cat had reached moments before, letting him in, only to find the kettle still warm from the tea he'd made a few hours earlier. Finding there was no need to get tea ready, he returned upstairs, leaving the door ajar for the cat to continue a mouse hunt, and headed to get dressed. Then finally, stepping out of the doorway into the garden, the rain kissed his cheek in welcome and surprise. The birds, watching loftily, whispered to each other: 'He's still here.'

The birds flew as he entered the garden but he waited and watched for them to return before working. It took time to summon up his new-found courage and to start to cut, making a tentative clearing here and there. First the undergrowth: burning the wasted thorn enabled him to see how to approach certain trees, those he'd considered removing first. These he marked with a bright yellow X, taking great joy in crossing each diagonal line with a perfect right angle. As he cleared his mind, he was able to keep returning outside and, from the simple act of first feeding the birds, the garden bloomed too. Gardening absorbed his attention, allowing him to surface above the fear. The sparrows' return alone had brought life, song and movement to the garden. The flowers were refreshed through precise pruning which attracted the bees and butterflies. Then as he rested, the birds watched with pleasure as the Gardener sat in the shade of the tallest bamboo. Seagulls also gathered to breed on the roof, mostly keeping noisily out of the way. The rock doves, however, were greedy and often cleared the feeder in a single morning, leaving little for the sparrows. The Gardener noticed this and bought two caged feeders, one with a plastic container for seed, one with mesh for fat-balls, in the hope this would resolve the situation. Dutifully, he filled each and hung them in the garden on the same frayed washing line, replacing those he'd placed several months before. The Gardener also stopped his drinking and started to write, just a little each day when the maelstrom allowed; when the fears retreated, when the sun dimmed. He needed the bread of angels. He needed this liberation. He needed this garden.

A few months before his return to the garden, he had been close to taking his own life. He had felt it burning inside like a cassette tape winding down to a desperate purity of a single-note ending. He'd imagined it as a monster you'd hear breathing in the dark with the sheets pulled up over your head or heard through a closed door. That fresh-pressed cotton, the flimsiest of armour but your only protection against the darkest dream, against the darkest nightmare that escapes from your head into the room. The Gardener had been lied to by the PTSD but untruth can be so beguiling and one day he could notice only its irreversible absence. The sower had cast her seed on stony ground, which now was blossoming into the lie of suicidal acceptability.

At his lowest, nothing was out of bounds. He just wanted quiet and stillness at any cost. He thought about walking into traffic at a road crossing but the only time he did this, he accidentally made eye contact with the truck driver and couldn't move off the pavement. The driver passed him unaware of the Gardener's unfulfilled wish. A few years earlier, his wife had called across that same crossing at a young man walking on the other side of the road. He had waited dutifully as they crossed and greeted her politely. She introduced the Gardener to the Boy and he smiled as the Gardener shook his outstretched hand. She worked with this Boy, he sat next to her, she explained, and mentioned how helpful he was to her when she wasn't well. He looked embarrassed, the Gardener thought, but they chatted for a while longer before there was a last goodbye and each resumed their intended walk.

Early in the morning, the Soldier, accompanied by others, rode into the village. They were behind the rapidly moving front line, now many miles ahead and only marked by slowly shifting pillars of smoke. The landscape was flat, unnaturally flat he felt. It seemed endless, each village the same as the one before with the next in sight through the heat haze. They had already noticed the truck, its tyres flattened, facing away from them in the middle of the single through road before they entered, and they wanted to take a closer look. A small crowd had gathered by the side of the road which the Soldier viewed with a knowing suspicion, his men moving forward to cover them. He stopped the other side of the truck and dismounted, his binoculars still hanging round his neck. Noticing a trail of blood, he traced it to the far side by a ditch. He scanned the horizon for movement, spotting something in the distance several miles away, but he had more to worry about than a few stray wounded escapees. He looked upwards hoping to see a familiar 'Eagle Owl' reconnaissance plane. He was disappointed by its absence. Cursing at the smell of blood, he turned and placed the binoculars back in their case, raising a fly mist as he stepped over several enemy bodies strewn across the road. Lifting the grubby canvas flap of the truck, he found several more. He motioned to a newly arrived junior officer who saluted somewhat excitedly and told him the villagers wished to bury the dead. The Soldier looked up ahead towards the distant smoke and told him to wait behind with some of the men for the rest of the company to catch up while he went ahead. 'Burn them,' he said, turning, and then, looking him in the eye, 'Better still, burn it all.' Only twenty-four hours later, that village and the one the Soldier was heading for had disappeared in charred ashes, efficiently 'solved' and buried underground.

The Boy crossed the border unnoticed under a moonless sky in the company of friends but led by strangers. The sense of alertness and imminent danger were new to him, but he kept his promises made to the others. At one village they rested, and as it grew hot, he watched a child feed some birds. Sparrows, the same as the ones at home, he thought. It gave him impetus to keep going. He misquoted to himself, 'Am I not worth more? If one should fall, will it not be known?' all the time looking down at the pale dust collecting on his feet.

The Gardener started to feel the cold when at last he reached the station crossing. It coincided with a pause between songs and, even with his headphones on, he pattern-picked sounds despite the noise about him. Reaching the other side, he removed his headphones and stood facing the railings as the sound of sparrows enveloped him. It took a few seconds but then he saw them hopping between branches not three feet away, bundles of feathers, brown and grey against the dusk and drying falling leaves. He smiled. He was oblivious to the traffic and the people passing him on the narrow path, except for one person who was whistling as he walked by. He thought, *How could they not notice this?* This marvel, nature happening outside of their cars, outside of their worlds, of their imaginations. He took out his phone, poked it through the metal bars and recorded the sparrows' conversations. After a while, he climbed the stairs of the footbridge to get a better look. The stubby trees were growing on a small patch of land perched above the rail line 25 feet below and, although not close enough to see them eye to eye as before, the sound was finer, less shrill against the traffic. As he carried on across the footbridge towards the trains the smile that had formed refused all attempts to leave.

A few weeks later, the unit was billeted in a shabby town. The Soldier, often bad-tempered now, drank frequently, the local spirit being cheap with an anaesthetic quality he craved. The work was difficult and they were frequently lectured on its necessity but he questioned this silently, and the lies he told himself to cover the lies others told him drove him to drink. One evening, he noticed a young woman flirting awkwardly with some of his men. She was an attractive redhead. The men saw him looking, stopped and ushered her over to his table. In the light, he noticed her eyes were reddened and she seemed scared through her smile. She sat in his lap and laughed as she drank but he could feel her trembling. They returned to his billet and fell asleep on the bed. Waking in the early hours, she pulled him close and they made love. It was his first time. By the time the early action alarm sounded, she was gone. He could still taste her. He dressed hurriedly, ill-prepared for the day's work and with just enough alcohol left in his system to numb the weakness of compassion.

One evening, while he was watching television, the Gardener's wife suddenly looked up and exclaimed, 'He's gone!'

'Who?' the Gardener replied, startled by the tearful tone of disbelief in her voice. She looked up from her phone, from the message she had just received.

'The boy from work, the one you met.' Then: 'He's gone to fight.' Her voice was breaking, incredulous, checking the phone screen again, desperate for an impossible change as tears filled her eyes. The Gardener asked her again who. 'You met him that one time – he waved at us and we crossed. I introduced you.' The Gardener searched his memory and remembered him, young and polite, and tried to comprehend how things like this were possible. A few months after the text, they sat and watched the airport CCTV video from the TV news several times, pausing it, confirming the long-suspected truth they didn't want to read or hear.

The station was crowded. It was that dangerous time of day. The Gardener had learned to tolerate rush hour but today was different: each time he moved closer to going home, the fears started to bite. Climbing the steps of the south entrance, he managed to get a quarter of the way across the concourse before his nerve failed. Moving at right angles to the flow of people was difficult but he made it to his known safe space under the first escalator opposite Platform 18. There was just a small railing he could lean on if the seats were occupied and it sheltered him from the crowds. He fingered the knot on his rucksack strap and counted slowly to ten, hating the way other passengers had barged into him on the main concourse moments before. Was he that invisible? Retreating behind his headphones, he was soon oblivious to the din around him. The rush of people appeared to slow, the colours drained and grew insignificant. He leaned back and closed his eyes as post-fear tiredness enveloped him once again.

The Soldier's reluctance to leave his room frightened him and he knew the look in his eyes scared his mother. He sometimes wondered whether she no longer recognised him. It had wormed its way to the surface and broken free in 1943 whilst he was home on leave. He had started shrieking in the early hours of the morning whilst it was still dark. His mother invited his fiancée to stay over the coming Christmas as a distraction. He welcomed her and his mood lifted for a while, but he suspected she was also relieved to be away from the city. He lay in bed remembering how he'd left in early summer of 1939, waving to her. He was still a child then, with a passion for nature and astronomy. He returned a man four years later. He wondered if his mother guessed he'd been injured by his experiences, which he would not speak about. He hoped she could console herself that he'd returned when so many others hadn't, and he whispered to himself that maybe she would wake with a smile. But often in his sleep he would hear nothing but that ugly word the army doctor had used: 'Kriegsneurose,' spoken by distorted or long-dead faces. He didn't think he should tell his mother this – or anyone else.

Whilst walking in the fields that afternoon, he realised it was time he told his mother the news. The following evening, he revealed he had been reassessed; his sick leave was over and he'd been called back to his unit. Unsurprisingly, the next day there was a knock at the door and the Soldier heard it being answered. There was a brief conversation and people entered through the hallway into the front room. He waited in the bedroom until he was summoned, straightened his hat and picked up his pack and rifle, exiting the room. His mother, as he had expected, cried and begged him not to leave. He removed her hands from his face, squeezed them in his own, kissed her and left – but not before picking up the bag of apples on the porch.

After several hours at the station, the Gardener finally managed to overcome his anxiety, leave his safe space and locate his train. Walking its full length, he discovered, to his great relief, that it wasn't full. He climbed aboard near the front. He wanted to be home and figured the front was slightly closer. Turning his gaze away from the window, he noticed a girl, talking to an older woman he assumed was her mother. The mother's voice was muffled but the daughter's voice, in contrast, cut bluntly through his headphones in a miserable monotone. He wanted her to leave the carriage but they had only just sat down. His first instinct was to flee. His horror was compounded at the next stop by the arrival of a heavily perfumed woman. He started to choke and with each breath felt he was drowning physically. He turned away and used his just-opened drink in a fruitless attempt to mask the now overwhelming smell. He didn't know her but instantly disliked everything about her: the large earrings, her short white hair, the brown bag she carried and each wrinkle lining her face. 'I'm walking a fucking minefield,' he said to himself as he gave in to temptation and emptied the can of energy drink. It started to snow as the woman finally left the train. He himself arrived home a short time later and, breaking the surface of those dark waters in which he felt he had been drowning, he took a deep breath and learned to swim again.

After being dropped off in a suburb of the town and completing his mother's mission, the Soldier walked down familiar streets. Round a corner, he came across the chaos of the railway station. There had been only a few night-time raids and leaflet drops, but people were clamouring to leave, presumably to stay with relatives in the surrounding countryside. They had often sent his city cousins back with crates of apples or potatoes, which ended up stacked six high, filling their small hallways, ready to be raided during the winter. But food was becoming more scarce now. He'd called in at his cousin's apartment on his way but wasn't sure whether the sack of older apples his mother had insisted he carry was more welcome than he was. He noticed, through the mass of grey and green, the glint of a military policeman's silver gorget approaching him. With steely eyes, the policeman examined his warrant and, turning, beckoned a colleague to come over. The other policeman led him to a train waiting on the far side of the station. He thanked the 'chained dog', an impolite nickname for a field policeman the unit always used in private, and climbed aboard moments before the train slowly left. After removing his pack, he sat on the plain green wooden slats and crossed his legs around the butt of his rifle so the bolt sat nestled under one knee. Leather sling gripped tight, he leaned forward, letting the cold muzzle caress his cheek, counted to three and closed his eyes.

The waves tumbled over the Gardener. He was aware, from the look on his wife's face, that the words were failing to leave his mouth in the order he'd intended to say them. They rolled around his mouth seeking liberation, only achieving fragmentation. As he stumbled, the cat scarpered into the hall and his wife looked in disbelief, lifting her head away from the words that had ensnared him. The Gardener, haunted by many shifting shadows, backed into the kitchen and was about to panic as his wife raised herself out of the chair. The waves engulfed him now. He shook violently, ripping his shirt in two at the front and howling, possessed with grief. She reached out and tried to hold him but this was too much. Her fingers felt like pins of burning steel piercing his skin. Then his mind finally broke free.

After three hours, the Soldier changed trains. The new station was even more chaotic but he noticed a general pattern: soldiers heading one way, civilians the other. Lost in a sea of grey, more examinations of papers followed and after a short wait another heavily laden train pulled into the platform. This time, the policeman stayed with him after noticing the streak of red, white and black ribbon and silver combat clasp pinned below his pocket. He seemed young and eager to hear any story of the front, but the train's arrival cut any account short. When the train stopped, the field policeman helpfully ordered an unwilling man from a full compartment to make room for him. After the train pulled out, the Soldier glanced away from the blackened station and noticed that the uniformed man seated opposite was staring at him. It wasn't a harsh stare, but rather passive, inquisitive. Yet what unnerved him most was the man's vague resemblance to his father. The moment their eyes met, the man leaned forward and said: 'If it wasn't for all this, your life may have been different, yes?'

These few words caught the Soldier off guard. This man was taking a risk; this was subversive, almost defeatist talk. The Soldier's eyes flicked around the carriage to see if anyone else had noticed. They hadn't, but danger still lurked. Maybe this man was unafraid or used to plain speaking. He looked back at his fresh uniform: the collar tabs, woven in machine BeVo style, utilitarian and cheap, new and blue. He was a medic.

'Yes,' the Soldier replied.

They started speaking freely, oblivious to their purpose or destination. The Soldier, for once, was keen to talk. The Doctor, he found out, was also on his way to the front but seemed more interested in the Soldier's childhood love of astronomy, rockets and nature. The Doctor removed his glasses and spoke of a shared love of walking in the mountains, adding that he had worked with children whom society deemed useless but within whom he had often recognised ability. As he spoke, the Doctor looked away and out of the window momentarily, pausing as if replaying a fond memory. Turning back, he smiled at the Soldier. After a while, they silently shared some lunch wrapped in brown paper.

After an hour or so, at the next station, the Doctor placed his hands on his knees and said, 'So this then is my stop.' As the train slowed, they both rose in concert, the Soldier, the taller of the two, reaching for the Doctor's bag held in the rope net behind him and putting it on the now-vacated seat. The Doctor shook the Soldier's hand in both of his and left. The Soldier followed his progress through the crowd until he could no longer tell him apart from all the others and sat back, rolling a coin between his fingers and wishing he'd asked the man for his name.

It took time for the Gardener to get to know his PTSD, like coming to know someone as a friend, someone who had first been imposed upon you, a family member you didn't like or could not trust. Some days, he was silent, diverting all his energy, needing it to stop the dam breaking. He knew the foundations were flawed, having been built on wet sand rather than rock. He could now see these things, like a landscape after a light snowfall, etched in binary shadow. Thankfully the birds spoke to him every day; he could hear them, even with the windows closed. They were reminding him: 'Tell the story, live it once again, and it will go.' He was scared. Every time he tried, he just sat there and cried, wept with the pain of the memories flooding back. Then one day, someone showed him how to extinguish the sun.

The Soldier sat watching his men, a cup of unpalatable but redemptive ersatz coffee clasped in his hands. He'd always disliked pompous officers, with their red-striped attitudes, never found at the front and always hiding behind the lines physically as well as in their thinking. They moved men around on the map with the nonchalance of passing a fruit bowl around a dining table in a brothel.

The Gardener's counsellor explained to him that his fear response was permanently switched on. She outlined the science to him. He'd read it all before. During one session, though, the counsellor asked a simple question: 'You talk about the pain being like a sun in your head, a sun that someone else has ignited.'

'Yes,' the Gardener replied.

'But can you walk round it?' she asked. 'See it from the other side.'

'I don't know,' he replied.

As he followed her fingers, crossed as if in a sign of peace, back and forth, he became aware, aware that what he had seen as a sun with a lifetime of billions of years wasn't really permanent. He looked at her and she stopped.

'Supposing what I'm looking at is just a frozen moment, like the film of an atom bomb on pause,' he said.

'Go on.'

'If I run it as a film, fast forward, it dies away, then backwards it reappears.' At that moment, he realised he had regained control, and he smiled.

Early the next morning, they moved out of their encampment and took up positions in the shallow trenches dug the day before. 'Not long to wait now,' he said as he looked at the child soldier next to him. He was young, maybe just fourteen, and completely lost. Then, as small stones started to slip down the side of the trench, in rhythm with the squeal of steel against wheel, they broke contact. With one hand grasping the Panzerfaust tube, the Soldier pulled the pin releasing the sight to be raised and lifted it with a single movement. The trigger armed, he waited. He had to be close. The tank broke through the hedge line followed by other khaki steel rhinoceroses. Deafened by a near miss, he stood up recklessly and fired. The tank ground to a halt just a few yards in front, burning furiously. He turned round, only to find part of his companion folded into the floor of the trench. The rest of the boy's body hung from the bushes behind. The Soldier ran towards the antitank ditches surrounding the village they'd passed the day before. He sat down and slid, the earth crumbling beneath him, stumbling into the darkness. He tried to control the equipment hanging from his belt and backpack, angling himself sideways in the hope that the blanket wrapping was just thick enough to muffle metal against metal.

Soon he found himself at the bottom of a short slope, crouched in a dip below a wall overrun by ferns and nettles. He was knee-deep in the drift of last autumn's leaves, surprised by the fragrances released as they were crushed underneath him. He remembered himself as a child, running through his grandfather's orchard in the neighbouring village, kicking and screaming as the banks of raked leaves became castles, moats and dragons. He wondered if that orchard was now blackened, leafless against the spring sky, awaiting a cooling, healing breath of late spring snow. After waiting for twenty minutes, all his senses attuned to the slightest rustle or twig snap, he left the sidewall, and made his way diagonally across the uneven stone path. Sooner than expected, he found an opening, over the closed half-gate and along the inside face of the hedge. He attended to the cuts, stings on his hands and leg, whilst everything within him was still screaming that he needed to reach home.

Stepping out of the corner shop, the Gardener almost tripped over a pigeon feasting obliviously on a half-empty crisp packet. As he walked home counting, he found the pavement was covered in cherry blossom. He crossed the road without looking for traffic, attention caught in an earlier century where he juxtaposed this spilt beauty with imagery of men laying waste to other lives on the insistence of others.

As it grew dark the Gardener decided to slug hunt. He couldn't have all that effort in tending and growing spoilt. He entered the garden, still warm from a full day of sun, to damp the paths and plants with water. He would wait for darkness before he struck. Back indoors making tea he realised how much he needed the garden but also how much the garden needed him. An ideal interdependency that he'd never achieved with a person before. He'd always longed to belong but even as a child he'd tasted difference in the way he interacted with the world. He watched the other children at school intently; learning to camouflage himself was a life-preserving exercise. He wondered, over the now half-empty cup, what price people were prepared to pay to find a home, to find belonging. The Boy, he wondered, what seed had been planted in him that had grown in such a perverse fashion? What borders had he crossed mentally and physically to forsake his heartbroken family for a belief; what zeal, what discipline was needed to leave his life behind? The Gardener simply could not imagine.

Later, out in the garden, he took to the task in hand. He searched under pot and leaf with his torch, even looking high into the bamboo for the tell-tale silver trail. Those he found he cut into pieces, which in turn attracted others to a feast and the attention of an early morning blackbird. He sat a while in the grey wicker garden chair, eyes skyward, hoping for a meteor to skim the atmosphere or burn bright as it passed. His thoughts were still with the Boy. No one spoke about him or where he was, just that he had left on a 'one-way ticket' with friends. The Gardener suspected he knew where the Boy was only because of their social media martyrdom and the polarised attention this drew in the press. The Boy it seemed was fated to be the last of them to pass,

2,824 miles away give or take a few. Would the Boy, in a moment of self-realisation, miss his family so desperately he'd wish to return or even be allowed to leave? The Gardener rose to go inside, thinking, *You've made your bed, now you just have to lie from it.*

The Gardener, now finally tired, diverted left at the top of the stairs into the back bedroom. Carefully hanging a coat in the doorway where a door should have been, he settled on the bed to write. When he had finished the cat sniffed the warm biro, battled it into submission and, satisfied with a quick win, settled next to him. That night the Gardener's dreams were of sand and tears, fears of lofty watchers waiting for a moment of exposure to strike, of never finding the way home.

There were no meteors that night, no flags waved, no moon to shine upon those faces of men waiting for the next day's killing.

The Soldier remembered, during that last touch of sun on his hand, the warmth of the bark beneath his fingertips, the sharpness of the pine needles, which seemed to taste blue, strewn beneath those now forgotten branches. His hand gripped the steel in the semi-darkness and he looked around hesitantly to see whether he'd been followed or was being watched. It seemed safe to keep going so he moved. He had become separated from his men while entering the wood a few hours before, out of breath, jumping the ditches between each row now softened by years of accumulation and frost, the silences broken only by a bird sound or the muffled footfall of bracken. He stopped and turned his head, tracing the pine cones, mostly eaten, robbed, torn apart like warm bread. He reached the next dip, the earth yielding to the slip. He felt behind him for his spade, undoing the thin leather strap and lifting the cold metal out of its holder. He sensed the urge to dig, to hide. But the smell of the first cut into the damp earth retrieved and then replayed a memory he'd prefer to have forgotten. He stopped, stamping the offending earth smooth. A bird flew low overhead. Its shadow startled him and he ducked down. It took him a while to resume the worn path, left by a deer or a fox. He scrabbled free of the confines of the cutout. The last rays of the sun, now lower in the sky, lingered gleefully on ferns, casting sawtooth shadows across his boots as he moved forward. He reached out as he advanced, touching trees, finding joy in the sap once soft but now hard enough for him to break away and pocket for later. He resumed his quest for a hidden space to lay his head, one with a view, one with a flavour of solitude.

Every day, the Gardener checked, with an air of inevitability, scanning online, searching for clues, images, anything that would lead to the only conclusion possible. He wanted to be the first to tell her; he didn't want her to hear it on the news or see the deserved comment. They had sat and counted them as they had fallen, one by one until he was the last one left. Why some people seemed impelled to build others' cathedrals of wickedness rather than rejoice in the world around them baffled the Gardener. He needed to know. He needed to see the finality.

The Soldier slept where he could for the following week, avoiding contact with anyone until he stopped exhausted on the outskirts of a small farm. In the quiet of a cowshed, he reached around for the gas mask container; the familiar, ribbed thin metal caressed now by dirty fingers. He pulled on the worn woven strap hoping it remained in one piece, and the catch released. The lid opened silently. He removed clip and cloth to retrieve the contents. Each object was always counted out so nothing was lost – an archive of objects, each valueless in itself but, when placed on a map, drew a timeline. Each was a memory, layered, pulling thoughts and deeds by their hair from the many. There they lay out in front of him, his coat acting as a tablecloth. After removing the wire retainer, he spilled the garish, thin tin badges which he'd retrieved from the bodies of the first people he'd killed, untrained conscripts running towards him with no guns, falling like wheat, scattered human chaff from a summer afternoon reaping. Next, the figurine wrapped in a newspaper, taken from a ruined town. Broken, one arm missing, lost on a November afternoon. Then the moleskin he used to wrap those few letters he'd received when the field-post finally caught up with them, dry and still. The spent copper bullet that had caught in his Zeltbahn and the sewing kit he'd used to mend the multiple holes in his uniform. Lastly, besides his papers, which he hastily buried in the soft earth, his personal kit, gritty soap and razor – and the hand-sewn handkerchief held in crisply creased greaseproof paper, both his and his fiancée's names embroidered on opposite corners so that, when folded, they rested upon each other. The handkerchief still retained her perfume. Breathing in her memory made him long for her touch.

The Gardener burst into the garden, with its new plants and vigour, towards the end of the summer, one September Saturday. He stopped and gasped in horror. The air was full of feathers. He followed them towards the body of a bird hanging from the feeder's bars. Fighting back tears, he tried in vain to free the still-warm dove. Her head was trapped and her neck broken in his absence. His wife came out to look. 'It's no one's fault,' she told him, but still he cried. He cried at the senselessness of it all, a loss he'd caused, feeling his guilt cut, letting the brambles regrow across his forehead. The Gardener carefully released the dove and placed her tenderly in a shoe box lined with tissue. After showing the dove to his wife and to be sniffed in recognition by the cat he went to the bottom of the garden. He moved the mint to one side, dug a hole, and awkwardly placed the box at the bottom, careful to add some broken tile over the top. He apologised one last time before the sun went down.

The Soldier was trapped. They'd advanced faster than he'd anticipated. In front of him, he could see several tanks and hear their decamped occupants. He skirted the copse and, finding a seemingly unguarded path, silently moved forward. Partway through, he froze. He could smell tobacco smoke: rough, impure, strong. There was a solitary guard in his way. Fixing the bayonet to his rifle, he hoped to catch him unawares. He silently pushed the safety off with his thumb and leapt from his cover. He raced sideways as the guard turned. They both fired simultaneously from the hip. The Soldier's single bullet caught the guard just below his jaw, snapping his chinstrap, liberating him of both life and a now red spinning helmet. As the guard fell, his finger locked around the trigger. The first bullet destroyed a clump of moss, but the second jolted the Soldier's right kneecap sideways through his trousers. He collapsed, the third passing through his armpit into his left lung, the rest clipping the branches behind and above him. The subsequent stillness was completed by a slow-motion shower of dried oak leaves and pain. Spitting sticky red dirt, he tried to move, but his leg bent unnaturally in front of him. He rolled and pulled himself upright against a tree. That was when the Soldier realised, not accepted, he would never be going home.

The Boy stepped outside the cool house and walked the length of the small walled garden. Feeling the cool stones beneath his worn sandals, he bowed, passing under the branches of ancient olive trees, and sat in one corner. The sun was the same sun that he had woken up to each day of his young life. The same sun that rose each day before he went to school, the same sun that would now be touching his mother's cheek. He chose to sit in the shade and waited. They soon came, loud and cheeky as usual, bobbing gratefully in the dust as he shared his breakfast with them. To him, they looked the same as those in his garden, those he'd chosen to leave behind and, looking up into the sky, he was grateful for this, his secret link with home.

The Soldier waited, propped against the tree, knowing home was a lifetime away. Through blurred eyes, he noticed a sparrow's nest that had fallen from the tree unseen moments earlier. Despite his numbness, the Soldier grieved for the broken eggs and for the fledglings lying motionless beside it. One of them moved. The Soldier held out his arm. Only stunned, it spread its wings and flew out of sight. As the breeze picked up and the last leaves fell, he thought of the farm, his mother and a story, the only story his father had told him of his war. How in the spring, they had caught up with the enemy trapped within a stone-walled cherry orchard, and during the firefight, leaves and blossom fell like snow, covering both the dead and the dying. Afterwards, they'd walked through the spilt pink, white and green, the future fruit cut down, stained and toppled before their time.

Three miles high above the warm desert, the drone circled. Two-thirds of the way into its mission, it soared asymmetrically, imperceptibly, and released its weaponry, and a short while later the car disappeared. The Boy who wanted to come home now never would. A few days later, the Gardener read the news online. His search over, he texted his wife to inform her. She already knew or felt she did. Later that day, they decided to write to his parents: the parents of a polite boy who always held the door open, who never swore or played video games, who simply made her tea.

The Gardener sat in the fuchsia-pink chair he'd tucked into the bamboo and waited for the birds. He sang gently to himself, drawing geometric shapes in the sand he'd spread on the patio that morning to comfort himself. In the shade, he remembered his grandfather again and the way he used to smile at him with that strange, distant look in his eyes. He now knew it was his grandfather watching over No Man's Land years later from the comfort and distance of his front room chair. He now knew he was safe.

The Soldier picked the cross off his chest, clasped it tight for a few moments and hummed a childhood song his mother often sang to him. He held the cross tight enough to make his forefinger and thumb bleed, before tossing it away in front of him. His rifle was sticking out of the ground at an absurd angle behind him, this time its bayonet impaling only leaf and soil. Each time he moved, he bled profusely. He heard voices approaching and realised he had one last choice of action. He pulled his pack closer and tugged the pair of stick grenades painfully from his belt. He pushed the wooden handles through a retaining strap first, trapping their wider heads. Turning the pack over, he unscrewed the hidden end caps, freeing from each the cord with a white porcelain ball at the end. Feeling for their tension against the strikers, he placed them in his palm with the cord between two fingers as if drawing back on a bow, and waited.

The autumn came and went and after a week's fevered preparation, the garden gradually became still. The Gardener checked it twice weekly, watering where needed. The winter sun, low above the station roof, reached only a third of the way up the sky. But the flowers still bloomed and, cutting gently, he welcomed them into his home to see out their last moments. He continued to fill the feeders over the winter and started to tidy and prepare for spring. As soon as it was warm and light enough, he'd open the window and lie awake to listen to the sparrows squabbling.

More guards, their rifles raised, bayonets fixed, approached the Soldier through the trees with twig and leaf telling steps. Surrounding him, they shouted or laughed. Seeing he was incapable of resistance, one of them turned, grinning, dropped to his knees and reached for the pack. It eventually came loose and the guard turned to the others and held it aloft just as the two grenades fell. The Soldier's hand opened simultaneously, spilling the two porcelain balls as if playing a game of marbles like a child. The enemy guard's face registered surprise for less than a second, and then disappeared.

The Soldier's final memory was the girl he'd first slept with, naked and ashamed, pushed by jeering and laughing comrades on the plank. She'd walked out, keeping her balance, with her arms raised, revealing a perfection he hadn't seen in the dark that night before. Horrified, the waves overwhelmed him, but when ordered to shoot, he did. For a split second he'd hesitated, but gripping under the magazine harder, closing his eyes, he fired. He had no option but to watch her fold, crumple, mouth open, a streak of scarlet silent on her lips as she fell back into the pit. His eyes opened. Feeling nothing but terror, he followed her, tumbling through the rows of bodies into his own intimate darkness.

The sparrows, now delighting in their new generations, watched from the lofty gutter as the Gardener opened the back door and started to tidy and tend. After a while he sat in his favourite place, tucked under the shelter of the largest bamboo. The birds played around him, squealing with glee, squabbling in and out of the bamboo and the nearby trees. It seemed to them that maybe none of them had ever really left the garden, their conversations renewing every day.

Even after the Gardener had risen from his seat to head indoors – and as dusk had fallen, the sparrows rising to the nearby roof and tree – joy remained.

The next morning when the Gardener woke, fear filled his heart. For a moment he waited, hovering within the event horizon of the usual nightmare from which he was fated to escape. But this day he realised he wasn't scared of what had gone before; those things were passing into abeyance. He was frightened of silence, an absence of song he'd grown so used to hearing; he was frightened of their leaving.

And this morning, the birds sang.

STANDARD CANDLES

DAMIAN SAWYER

The bitter, gusting wind threatens to knock her off her feet, but she braces herself against it, struggling on up the coastal path to the headland. The sea spray and the light rain are indistinguishable. On days like this she wishes she was still up to baking her own bread. Instead, twice weekly she makes this journey to the village, trading her skill at mending for a few freshly baked rolls. Everyone seems so young there, now. It stirs her heart to see the joy in their faces, and to be greeted warmly by them all. The women would bring food to her if she would let them, but she needs this time away from her home to remind her that, even at her age, life goes on.

Near the crest of the high cliff, the path veers inland, cutting through tangled undergrowth. Gorse and thick bramble enclose it on both sides, making the turn easy to miss, but her feet know their way through years of experience. She is thankful for that, as her aged eyes are not much use in the fading light of sunset. She longs for warmer days, but her shivering is only partly due to the cold. Is she just imagining that she can hear animals stirring among the gorse and briar? The wind makes the bushes move as if they themselves were monstrous creatures, snatching at her. She's glad when she reaches the open grass of the low hills.

A sudden, unearthly cry rings out and she turns in shock, heart racing, until she realises it's just a fox. She always finds their call disturbing, sounding so much like a crying baby that her heart yearns to go out into the night to find the poor, lost child. She turns back and continues on her way, but after a while she feels uncertain; is she still heading in the right direction? The slope of the ground beneath her aching feet seems different, unfamiliar. Should she turn, and if so, which way? The fox calls out again, but she can't even tell which direction it's in. For all she knows she could have turned right around and be heading back towards the shore.

Warily, she crests another hill. What is that? There, below her, some way to her left, is a tiny but bright light; a literal glimmer of hope. Her fears are suddenly gone, and she heads straight towards it, not doubting for a moment what it signifies. As she reaches her small cottage, the fox cries out once more, far behind her, but it cannot unsettle her now. She lifts the latch, opening the door to her home, where the light of that one small candle...

... floods her room; bright, eye-watering autumn sunlight, blazing through the thin curtain that barely covers the one small window. The cry rings out again; Shannon in her cot, barely catching her breath before launching into the next wail. Another morning, Lianne feeling as burned out as the tealight candle she had lit the evening before. She hastily bins its remains. Candles are not strictly allowed in the hostel, but then neither are drugs or alcohol, and they seem to find their way in anyway.

Morning nappy change: how could anyone eat breakfast after that? Bottle made up, cooled down, temperature tested. She hates the smell of the drops of baby milk on her wrist, and Shannon is still crying. Bottle does the trick, mother cradling her precious daughter, each of them half-asleep.

Both dressed, Shannon now fast asleep in her pushchair, Lianne wheels it through to the hostel caff. The smell of bacon and eggs assaults her. She used to love that smell. Now it's too closely linked with the nervous glances and simmering tensions of hostel life. Most of the residents are alright, but there are always the few, unable to cope with relying on the charity of strangers, who resort to intimidation, unwanted advances or violence. She hopes her baby will keep her safe from all of that. No fry-up for her nowadays, just cereal and milk, and – thank goodness – hot black coffee.

It's like Lianne never left the playground. There are five of them, other young mums or mums-to-be, living in the hostel. They cluster outside the caff, in reception. Denise is their leader, by virtue of being the most brash and outrageous. Two days ago she broke up with the latest in a long string of lovers, by quite literally kicking him out. He was too ashamed to get the police involved. 'Hey, Lianne!' Denise shouts over her toddler, who she hasn't even noticed is halfway to escaping his pushchair. 'You should get yourself some lovin', girl!' She holds her arms out as if embracing someone, moves her hips and groans suggestively, and the other four laugh. Lianne smiles, but only in embarrassment. Inside she feels sick. She knows she will never fit in with their little group. Even if she tried, they would turn on her in an instant, spite her just for some twisted sort of entertainment. She doesn't want to end up like them; using people just to dull the pain, boredom and loneliness.

When she is with the other girls while Denise isn't around, they seem like they could be really good friends. Lianne can't get her head around that; how someone can be such a different person depending on whether a certain individual is there or not. Their little gang is a fellowship born from enduring the callousness of men, and the judgemental looks from so many people. Lianne chooses to bear those looks alone, but still imagines she hears people's unvoiced comments: 'How can she care for a baby when she can't even get a flat of her own?' 'Too young to be raising a child – I expect she sleeps around. What a waste of a life.' 'Poor kid, what sort of future will she have with a mum like that?'

She needs a break from the hostel, so she takes Shannon out to the park. It's a fair walk, but worth it just to sit watching the ducks and the sun-brightened trees reflected in the lake in red and yellow splendour. Shannon is awake and gurgling to herself.

'Look, Shannie, duck-ducks!' Lianne says to her, then

in a silly voice, 'Quack-quack!' Shannon laughs, so she says it again.

As much as she loves these times, Lianne wishes there was someone to share them with. Not Shannon's dad. He was out of the picture months ago, and good riddance to him. As usual, there are a few couples walking by the lakeside, some with kids, most just enraptured by each other's company. Lianne wonders how many of them realise what heartbreak feels like, how love can become a toxic thing.

'Mind if I sit here?' a voice asks. It's a young woman about Lianne's own age, perhaps a few years older.

Something snaps in Lianne's mind. Can't she even have five minutes to herself? 'Have your bench,' she says, standing abruptly, then storms off, the pushchair bouncing slightly on the uneven path. Shannon starts crying.

Back at the hostel that evening, with Shannon settled for the night, her magnolia-walled room feels like a prison cell. Lianne wonders why she was so angry at the stranger. If only she could find her, apologise... but then what would she say? She doesn't even know why she snapped at her. She lights another tealight, almost as if it were a penance. Lying in bed, she watches the flame until sleep takes her.

The sanctuary is a glorious place, not with bright light but with shadows and stillness. Outside the World goes on in its bustle and turmoil. Here, a single flame brings life to the stone walls and a sense of calm to the soul. Occasionally it flickers to one side for a moment, as if an unseen angel had breathed upon it.

'We keep this flame burning as a reminder of what our Lord said.' The abbess, bent almost double by old age, is instructing her. '"You are the light of the World; a village on a hill, whose lights shine in the night; a lamp, uncovered, lighting up the whole room." The World can be a dark place, like this room, but one small light can transform it. Let your light shine before others and the darkness cannot stand against it.'

'But what is our light?' she asks in response. 'What if the World should seek to put it out?' Inwardly, she is doubting her calling to the sisterhood. Learning doesn't come easy to her. If her training is this much of a struggle, will she be strong enough to honour the vows she hopes to take?

The abbess takes a reed from a receptacle nearby, holds it before her. 'This is our life,' she says solemnly, 'a dead thing, dark and discarded until...' and she lights it from the almost-spent candle. 'We carry the flame; not our own, but that pure light that first shone in Eden. We hold it for this short time on Earth and...' she lights the new candle, 'in acts of kindness, we ignite in others' hearts the glory that is to come. It is our privilege to shine for our brief lives with love towards all who need help in the darkness. And then...' she blows out the reed's tiny flame, 'we are gone from this place and we ascend.' The abbess smiles, beatifically.

As the novice meditates on the lesson and regards the time-worn visage before her, she realises that the abbess's light is soon to depart. The smoke is rising in fragrant curls towards Heaven...

... and Lianne awakens to the sickly-sweet smell of cannabis being smoked in one of the adjacent rooms.

It's bitterly cold outside, with a sharp breeze and frequent showers. Even so, Lianne can't stand to be stuck inside all day, so after breakfast she heads off out, grateful for her winter coat. Shannon looks miserable, trapped in the bubble of the pushchair's raincover. First stop: the pound shop. Lianne's money is almost all gone, nappies being the biggest expense. She goes straight to a particular shelf, and thankfully they have what she wants. Forty tealight candles for a pound – more than a month's worth.

Out from the shop and through the rain towards the park. Shannon starts crying in that particular way that usually indicates a smelly nappy. Off to the public loos, then. Lianne hates bringing Shannon in here. The changing table is always cold, even more so on such a chilly day. The stale smell, the chill in the air, Shannon screaming at the ordeal; it's what nightmares are made of. 'What did I do to deserve this?' Lianne mutters to herself, then involuntarily thinks, *Fell in love... idiot!*

Once Shannon is dressed again, Lianne hugs and rocks her gently while her last few sobs subside. 'There, that wasn't so bad, was it? All done now!' Shannon yawns as if in agreement as she is fastened back into the pushchair.

The lake is as grey and choppy as the clouds scudding overhead. Even the ducks can't be bothered to come quacking round in anticipation of being fed. *They've got more sense than me*, Lianne thinks. For half an hour she sits braving the freezing air, gently moving the pushchair back and forth to keep Shannon settled. She's shivering now, but still won't admit defeat. At least the weather is consistent. Hostel life is unpredictable, demoralising and at times terrifying. Lianne understands why some people prefer to sleep out on the streets, even on days like this.

'Hi there. Listen, do you want a cuppa? I'll buy you one.' It's that woman again. Lianne tenses up with the recollection of their last meeting. The opportunity to make amends is tempered by her fear of being judged, but the chance to escape the biting cold is stronger than either of these.

'Okay,' she says, 'thanks.' She walks in silence, head down, towards the park's small coffee shop.

The woman beside her says, 'It's okay, we don't need to talk. You look like you need warming up.'

Lianne tries desperately to work this out – does the woman think she's out on the streets? Perhaps she just feels pity for her; that's the last thing she needs. Is it some twisted sort of mothering complex? Does she fancy her? She supposes that these days having a baby isn't enough to show that she's not that way inclined. Whatever this woman thinks she's getting out of this, Lianne decides to just have her drink and then leave.

They find a table far enough from the door to avoid the bitter breeze that blows in whenever it opens. 'Tea please, two sugars,' Lianne says when asked. She's trying not to stare, to assess the woman, but really she is just glad to be out of the cold.

The woman returns with their drinks. 'I'm Lucinda,' she says.

'Sounds old-fashioned,' Lianne replies, unthinking.

Lucinda smiles. 'My dad really likes the name.'

'Hm. It's okay I guess. I'm Lianne.' She tries to sip her tea – still too hot – then adds, 'And this is Shannon.' The baby is stirring. Lianne folds back the raincover.

'She's gorgeous, isn't she?' Lucinda says, and Lianne can't help feeling suspicious. Why this sudden interest in her daughter?

'What's this about?' she asks, a hint of yesterday's aggression returning to her voice. 'What do you want from me?'

'Nothing,' Lucinda replies, and Lianne is thrown by the honesty in the woman's face. 'You just look like you need a friend. If you prefer, I'll sit at another table, but have your cup of tea anyway. Spend some time in the warm and dry. Really, I don't mean to intrude.'

Lianne doesn't know how to deal with this; after all the people who have hurt her, she finds it difficult to believe someone could be so genuine, with no agenda and no plan to use her somehow. 'Sorry,' she says reluctantly.

'It's okay; you're on your own, I get that. It can't be easy. Do you mind if we chat? As much or as little as you want; I won't be upset if you say you've just had enough.'

'Okay,' Lianne replies, 'can't do any harm, I s'pose.' Shannon is playing with her pushchair toys, mumbling to herself.

'I guess her dad's not around?' Lucinda asks.

'No, he made tracks when I told him I was pregnant.' The bitterness is plain in her voice. 'Couldn't leave me fast enough.'

'Have you got any family?'

Lianne shakes her head. 'Just my mum, but she doesn't want to know me.'

'I'm so sorry, that's got to be really difficult.'

'Doesn't matter. There's just Shannon and me now.' Shannon looks round at the mention of her name and smiles. 'Yeah, little miss, just you and me,' Lianne says.

'No friends?'

Lianne shakes her head. 'Lost touch with everyone after we finished high school, and I've not really made any friends since then. S'pose some of my schoolfriends must be married by now. Might even have their own babies, too.' *And their own houses*, she thinks jealously.

As if she could hear these thoughts, Lucinda asks, 'Do you have your own place?'

'No, I'm on the council waiting list. Mum kicked me out, so I had to go into a hostel. Been there a month now, and my support worker says it'll be two more before I get a place. I just feel so useless; no home, no job. No man, but maybe that's not such a bad thing.' Lianne doesn't know why she's suddenly able to talk so freely.

Lucinda takes a notepad and pen from her handbag, and starts writing. 'Like I said, I don't want to intrude – you've got enough to deal with as it is – but if you need anything, just call me.' She rips out the page that she has written her mobile number on, and hands it to Lianne. 'Even if you just want another chat, any time you want.'

Lianne still feels uneasy, so she asks, 'Are you some sort of social worker?'

'No,' Lucinda says, 'I'm just a friend who'll be there if you need one. Do you have a phone so I can keep in touch?'

'Can't afford one.' Despite her doubts, there's a nagging feeling in Lianne's mind: this 'Lucinda' could just be someone to talk to when everything gets a bit too much. 'I suppose you could call the hostel.' She gives the details so that Lucinda can note them down.

Shannon gives a half-hearted cry, the kind that could easily escalate to a full-blown tantrum, so Lianne gets her out of the pushchair. She looks around eagerly, then tries to grab her mum's drink. 'No you don't,' Lianne tells her, moving the cup out of her reach. She gets a toy out of the changing bag – a bright, multi-coloured rabbit. Shannon waves her arms and shouts in excitement, grabs the toy then hums to herself as she shakes it.

'Someone's wide awake,' Lucinda says.

'Yeah, full of energy.' Something occurs to Lianne:

'How about you? Have you got kids?' Lucinda shakes her head. 'Any family?'

Lucinda smiles. 'I spend time with my dad every now and then.'

'My dad died when I was eleven. Mum couldn't cope. That's when we started arguing. It's like she became a different person; maybe in some twisted way she blamed me for Dad not being around.'

'Sorry,' Lucinda says, and it looks like she means it.

'Ancient history now,' Lianne says, then after a brief pause, 'but I don't normally talk about it.'

'Well, I'm glad you feel okay to talk to me now.'

Lianne watches Shannon, who's now fascinated by the rabbit's ears. Gathering her courage, she says, 'I'm sorry about yesterday, for snapping at you.'

'Don't worry,' Lucinda replies. 'No harm done.'

'It's just... I'm so used to having to get through things on my own.'

'You don't have to. Just call me if it's too much.'

Lianne nods distractedly. At that point, Shannon hiccups loudly.

They both laugh, making Shannon look up in surprise.

After a good couple of hours together, it's back to the hostel in time for dinner, but even the accusing voices in Lianne's head are silent now. Let people think whatever they want. At least she knows that she's found a friend, and doesn't have to go through all this on her own. Settling down that evening, she lights the first of her new pack of tealights. Its flame seems brighter and warmer tonight.

She doesn't mind the jolting ride or the slightly stale smell of the bus. It's worth half an hour of this, knowing that at the end she'll be meeting her friends. Her friends! So strange to think that at long last she has been accepted by the very ones who used to mock her. Now she's beaming, wearing her best dress, and out to have some fun. Maybe even meet a boy, who knows...

The streetlights are just switching on in the early spring chill. No rain, so that's a blessing. On through the darkening streets, past cars and people walking, mostly heading in the opposite direction, back from the factories to their homes. She thinks of their lives of work and austerity, never daring to hope for anything better. But this is a new time, a chance for her generation to start living, and fifteen is a wonderful age to be.

She gets disapproving stares from the old lady in the seat opposite. Maybe her yellow dress is too bright, or the neckline a bit too low. Perhaps her hair is styled too extravagantly. She doesn't care; tonight is a night to enjoy herself. I bet she had fun when she was young, *she thinks, and resolves never to grow so old and miserable. The old dear rings the bell, waits for the bus to stop, then hobbles slowly to the exit. An involuntary thought surfaces:* Get a move on, I don't want to be late.

Finally, the bus reaches the seafront, and she hops down the steps to the pavement. The bus pulls away noisily with a blast of smoke from the exhaust. She looks around eagerly for her friends. No sign of them, so she checks her watch. Ten minutes early. They'll be here soon.

She can hear the music from the fairground, their destination for the evening, just a few minutes' walk from the bus stop. She watches the bright lights flashing, the big wheel turning then stopping, turning again. She looks around again for her friends. A group of young people go past, laughing noisily; they are a few years older than her of course, and she can't help noticing that each girl has a boy's arm around her.

Twenty minutes later, and the fairground's lights are starting to lose their appeal. She doesn't understand. Why haven't they arrived? Her feet are starting to ache from standing still for too long. She paces back and forth, occasional passers-by casting concerned looks her way.

She's sure they said to meet here, and certain it was to be six-thirty. She runs the conversation over in her mind: Angie inviting her, spelling out the details, smiling all the time. 'That's settled, then!' she had said. 'See you Thursday night!' Then she recalls the bell ringing for lessons, and Angie and her gang laughing.

She thought they were excited for the night out. Now she realises that once again they were laughing at her. She feels so stupid, so worthless, all the things that they think she is. The tears come unbidden, making her even more ashamed. She hastily uses her handkerchief to rub off her mascara before it can run. She doesn't want to get the bus home yet, doesn't want her mum to know about this.

Instead, she walks dejectedly away from the funfair and towards the pier.

It's really dark tonight. It's out of season, so there's no show in the pavilion. She walks the length of the pier, listening to the gentle crash of the waves against its supports. She wishes they were more violent, more stormy, like the emotions raging inside her. Looking over the railing, she can barely see the water. She wants to jump into it, let the cold blackness swallow her. Would a fall from this height kill her? She wouldn't want to jump only to be swept back and forth like a piece of driftwood. She wants the pain, the rejection, the shame of it all to disappear, to be gone in an instant, just to end...

Then she sees something. Off to her left, up in the sky above the water is a light. It's not cold like the streetlights, not frozen in place like some distant star. It moves, warm and yellow, floating in a bewildering course up and out to sea. She's fascinated, and can't take her eyes off it. She watches until it's no longer visible, then just as she starts back towards the promenade, she sees another. It rises from the beach; a flicker, then a light, sharply climbing then meandering slowly out over the waves.

Once off the pier, she heads over towards the place these strange lights are coming from. She steps down onto the sand, heedless of her best shoes, and sees a girl around her age, standing watching the receding glow. Once it is no longer discernible, the girl kneels, strikes a match. It illuminates a football-sized paper globe, some little container below it catching the flame. The girl blows the match out, lifts the globe then releases it to fly into the night sky. It rises like a little hot air balloon. She walks towards the girl and calls out, 'Hello?'

The girl turns and says, 'Hello there.'

'Those lights are beautiful! What are they?'

'They're sky lanterns. My father got them for me. They're from China. Aren't they great?'

'I've never seen anything like them.'

They stand together, watching the lantern float lazily away over the sea until it's no longer visible.

'I've got two left,' the girl says. 'How about lighting one each? We could have a race.'

'That's a great idea, thanks.'

So they light their lanterns, the flames illuminating their smiles, count 'Three, two, one...' and release them at the same time.

They watch the lights float away into the night, weaving around each other as if they were dancing. The night somehow doesn't seem as dark now. It doesn't matter whose lantern wins the race. They both watch, enraptured. The only music is the gentle swish, over and over; the sound of the waves...

... is the noise of cars driving past outside, in the rain. Lianne lies awake for a good hour, listening. It's like the hostel has been transformed overnight. She's never known it to be this peaceful.

After a while, with Shannon still sleeping, she goes to the shared kitchen to make herself a cuppa. When she gets back it's still only 6 a.m. She watches her daughter sleeping, wriggling now and pulling faces. 'What are you dreaming about?' she whispers. Just a few minutes later, Shannon wakes up screaming.

8:15 a.m. Nappy change, bottle, hugs; all have failed to calm Shannon down. She didn't have an arm or a leg trapped between the bars of her cot, doesn't have a temperature, doesn't look unwell. Lianne is at a complete loss. Head pounding, she doesn't know what else she can do, so reluctantly she lays Shannon back in her cot, hoping she'll just cry herself back to sleep. Then there's a hammering on her door.

The guy from the next room is there, an angry scowl on his face. 'My girlfriend's in my room. She needs to sleep, so shut that baby up!' It's an order. He's obviously used to always getting his own way.

'How?' Lianne asks. 'There's no off switch, you know.' She steps into the corridor and closes the door behind her, hoping Shannon doesn't get even more distraught.

'I don't care what you have to do, just shut it up!'

He starts to storm off down the corridor towards the main entrance. Lianne swears out loud at his back. As soon as he turns around again she knows that she has made a mistake.

'*What did you say?*' he shouts, his face now inches from hers. She winces at the smell of his breath, but stands her ground.

'You heard me,' she replies, calmly now. She knows he's the unreasonable one, the one who's being stupid, and that what she said was justified – that is, until his fist smashes into her eye.

Time seems to have stopped. That one moment of shock has broken it somehow. As if in a sequence of images in a slideshow, Lianne is aware of:

the crack of the impact...

her head snapping back...

her body slamming against the door, forcing it open...

falling to the ground, hitting her head on the floor...

the door swinging shut, now she's fallen through it...

Shannon somehow managing to scream even louder than before...

The pain seems to arrive hours later, but in reality it's less than two minutes. The hostel's duty manager knocks on her door and calls her name.

'Are you alright?'

Even that gentle knock terrifies her. Shannon has mysteriously gone quiet, just watching her now as if sensing her mum's suffering. Lianne stands unsteadily. She trembles uncontrollably as, warily, she opens the door.

The paramedic interrogates her; that's what it feels like.

'Did you bang your head?'

'Yes.'

'Were you knocked unconscious?' He's shining a light in her unbruised eye.

'No, I don't think so.'

'Do you feel sick at all?'

Yes, she thinks; sick of what's happened to me, sick of this place, sick of my sorry excuse for a life. But what she says is, 'No.'

Verdict: no need to go to hospital. Lianne's heart sinks. At least there she would have been safe.

Half an hour later, her support worker, hastily called in, is holding Shannon and walks with Lianne to the bathroom. Lianne tries to avoid looking at herself in the mirror, her left eye now swollen so much that she can barely open it. She tries to convince herself that it can't be all that bad, glances at her reflection; it's worse than she had dreaded. She hates herself for looking so awful, and bursts into tears, which make her battered eye sting even more.

The policewoman means well.

'I'm sorry, I know it was horrible having to go through it all, but we need to build a strong case so we can take it further. We've spoken to some of the other residents; several of them heard shouting and banging.' (Lianne is instantly back there again... his fist, the door, her head hitting the floor...) 'We're still holding him at the station, but he's likely to be released on bail, either today or tomorrow. We'll get back to you if we need any more info.'

The hostel manager says, 'It's going to take a while to sort this out. Sorry, but we can't move him straight away, and we can't move you either; we don't have any spare rooms.' (Lianne imagines doing a 'Denise' on him, kicking him out herself. If only it were that easy.)

Her support worker has stayed with her all morning. She says, 'Is there someone you could stay with, just for a couple of days until we can arrange for him to be transferred to another hostel?'

Lianne shakes her head and says, 'No, there's no one,' but then she remembers. 'Can I make a phone call?'

Lianne waits in reception. The changing bag hanging from her shoulder is packed solidly now with the addition of her own few items of clothing. She's rocking Shannon back and forth in her pushchair. Milk powder, bottles and steriliser are in a large carrier bag beside her, along with Shannon's playmat. Denise walks over, pushchair and chocolate-smeared toddler preceding her. Shannon thinks, *Please, no, not on top of this...* The last thing she wants is any 'advice' from Denise.

'You alright?' The words seem incongruous, coming in such a gentle way from this normally brash woman. 'I ran to reception when I heard the fight...' (*Not much of a fight*, Lianne thinks.) 'I let them know what was happening. Want me to give him a good kicking? Somewhere it'll really hurt?' She means it, of course.

'No,' Lianne replies, 'I'll be okay.' She doesn't believe it. How could anything ever be okay? Denise's boy is blowing raspberries at Shannon. She doesn't look impressed.

'Thanks,' Lianne says to Denise. 'My friend's on her way to pick me up.'

Denise nods. 'You take care of yourself, girl, and this little lady, of course.' She tickles Shannon's side, making her squeal with laughter. Lianne smiles; Denise has let the mask of her outrageousness drop. The real Denise is as different to who she seems to be as those other girls who hang around with her. 'See ya soon,' Denise says, then to her boy, 'Conor, say bye-bye.' He blows another raspberry in response. Denise sighs in exasperation and heads over to the caff.

Just then, the buzzer rings and Lianne looks up to see Lucinda at the front door. 'Oh, Lianne...' she says as she walks over and hugs her. Lianne starts crying again. 'Come on, let's get you out of here. I've borrowed a car seat and a travel cot, and there's a spare bedroom at my place. You're welcome to stay there as long as you need to.'

Lianne laughs through her tears. 'Can't stay too long or I'll lose my place on the waiting list.'

'Just however long you can, then.'

Shannon loves the journey. It's the first time she's been in a car. Her eyes are wide, watching the world speed by.

'I'm really sorry, putting you out like this,' Lianne says.

'No problem. I wouldn't want you to have to stay there tonight after what happened. You did the right thing calling me.'

'I haven't even got any money to go towards petrol.'

'Don't worry about it; I've only got myself to look after, you've got madam there. I expect she could do with a break from the hostel, too.'

Lucinda's house is a modest semi-detached in a leafy cul-de-sac, not far from the park. The living room runs the length of the house, with pleasant apple-green walls. Not magnolia, thank goodness. There are a few picturesque watercolour paintings on the walls, a comfy sofa and chairs, but to Lianne's surprise, no TV. 'I never thought much of it. I prefer the radio,' Lucinda says when she asks. Lianne has to admit that it's very peaceful here with the music filling the room. Shannon is on her playmat, quite happy rocking back and forth. 'It won't be long until she can turn herself over,' Lucinda remarks. 'There'll be no stopping her after that!'

Lianne asks, 'Do you want kids?'

'I would, but I can't have children,' Lucinda replies, her voice tinged with sadness.

'Sorry, I didn't mean to pry.' Lianne looks away, wishing she hadn't asked.

'It's alright. At least I know.'

The few seconds of silence are unbearable, but even so it takes a lot for Lianne to ask, 'No boyfriend?'

'No... but that's okay too.'

'But you've got a job, right? You must have, to be living here.'

'Yes, I'm a carer.'

'That makes sense; you've got the right personality for it.'

'I hope so. How are you feeling now?'

'Sick. My eye's killing me. But it's what happened more than the pain. You know, that feeling when the whole world seems to collapse on you?'

'I know. It's normal to feel that way after such a shock. Things will get better, I promise you.'

'Yeah, eventually, I guess...' Lianne says, then lapses into silence.

Lianne helps prepare dinner – shepherd's pie. Lucinda chops the onions to avoid them making Lianne cry even more. Lianne peels and chops the potatoes.

'You could be a professional,' Lucinda comments. 'Do you enjoy cooking?'

'Don't get much of a chance. Breakfast and dinner are provided at the hostel; all I have to sort out is lunches. There's a shared kitchen, but most of the time I don't have the money or the energy to cook anything.'

'That's a shame. Food tastes better when you cook it yourself.'

Once dinner is in the oven, they sit in the living room watching the sun set behind the small but well-tended back garden. Lianne asks if Lucinda would like to hold Shannon.

'Thanks,' she replies gladly. 'Hiya, little lady, aren't you beautiful!' she says as she takes her in her arms. Shannon looks unsure, but then laughs as Lucinda bounces her on her knee and sings nonsense to her. For Lianne it's a strange experience: seeing her child with someone else means she can see her as she truly is, without the constant pressure and expectation of being 'Mum'. The smell of the shepherd's pie fills the house.

After dinner, it's time for Shannon to have her bottle. Lianne finds it so much better preparing it in a pleasant environment, without having to hold Shannon at the same time. By eight o'clock she is fast asleep in the travel cot in the living room. A small table lamp gives sufficient light without being bright enough to wake her.

Lucinda places their cups of tea on the coffee table. 'I'll have to leave early tomorrow,' she says. 'I'm spending the day with my dad. You're welcome to stay here. Let me get you the spare key in case you want to go out. Help yourself to any food in the cupboards and fridge.'

'Thanks again,' Lianne says.

When Lucinda returns, she doesn't just have the key. Having handed that over, she says, 'This is something I do every night.' She shows Lianne a tealight candle.

'What? You light candles? I do that too, one a night!'

'Do you want to light this one?' Lucinda asks. Lianne nods, still amazed. 'Here,' Lucinda says, 'I put it on the windowsill, by the garden.'

Lianne takes the offered matches, strikes one, lights the candle, blows the match out and puts it in the bin, just like she does every night in her room at the hostel. They sit in the armchairs and watch the flame while they sip their tea.

'What are the chances?' Lianne says. 'We go to the same park, we both light candles. It's almost like we're sisters.'

'And you let me help you out when you needed it. We've shared a meal as well, and in some cultures that would make us family.'

'I've never had a sister before,' Lianne says, smiling.

'And I've never had a niece,' Lucinda replies, gesturing towards the travel cot.

'One day I'll have my own house,' Lianne says. 'Then you can come and visit us. Being here makes it feel more real to me, less like a dream that won't ever happen.'

'You'll get there. A day will come when you'll look back on your time in the hostel and see it was just a temporary phase.'

'Hope so,' Lianne says, nodding.

'How do you feel about what happened today?' Lucinda asks.

'Terrible,' Lianne replies. 'Don't know how I'll cope when I have to go back there.'

'It really hurts, right? I don't mean the physical pain, I mean inside.'

'Yeah.'

'Do you know why?'

'What do you mean?'

'Why it hurts so much – not just today; everything that's gone wrong for you, like Shannon's dad leaving you.'

'I guess it just feels so unfair. I shouldn't have to be on my own, coping with all of this.'

'You know things should be better, but they aren't. Let me show you something.' Lucinda puts her cup down. 'Come over to the window.'

Lianne is puzzled; it's dark outside now. What could there be to see? Even so, she gets up and walks over.

'Look up. What do you see?'

'The stars,' Lianne says.

'Is that all?'

'Yeah, just the stars – why?'

'You don't see the darkness, you see those tiny little points of light. But in your life right now, all you notice is the darkness. And you know there's got to be some sort of light there somewhere, but you can't see it.'

'I guess so...'

'That's why you light your candles; it's why I do it too. Keeping that light alive inside, despite all the ways the World tries to put it out. We light the candles to remind ourselves the darkness can never overcome even such a small, fragile flame.'

'That's beautiful,' Lianne says, 'and maybe a bit sad as well...'

'You know, my dad sometimes talks to me about the stars. He knows a lot about them. There are some that are called "standard candles". The scientists know from studying their light that they have to generate a certain brightness; like our tealights, each one always shines with the same amount of light. So they use them to map the heavens. If they look brighter, they're closer. If they're dimmer, they're further away.'

'Uh-huh, I get it,' Lianne says.

'People are a bit like that. We're meant to shine. It's like with Shannon; she doesn't need to do anything, just being there is enough. She's a bright little light in your life.'

Lianne is close to tears. 'Yeah, I never dreamed I could have anything so precious. She's my light alright.'

'But don't you see, you're her light as well?' Lianne shakes her head, but Lucinda continues. 'I see it in her eyes when she looks at you. Don't you have good memories from when you were young, spending time with your mum and dad? Feeling that they were always there for you, that they were all you ever needed?'

Lianne smiles. 'Yeah, we had some great times.'

'Well, that's how Shannon feels now about you.'

'S'pose I've just been doing what I have to, just getting through, waiting for things to get better. Never really had a chance to think about it.' She stares at the candle flame shining on the windowsill, just in front of her.

'Every person can be a blessing just by being there. Babies do it without even knowing. And what hurts most of all is when people turn that blessing into a curse, when they use it against us.'

'Like my boyfriend ditching me?' Lianne still can't bring herself to say his name. 'And my mum disowning me?'

'Yes,' Lucinda says, 'that's what really hurts. How can someone who's shown you love be so cold towards you? They've chosen to be so distant from what they should be, and so distant from you, that their light seems as black as night. Don't keep staring into that darkness. Find the standard candles: the ones who stay true to you, who keep close to you, and keep caring. Let them bring light into your life. Shannon does, I know, and I hope I do too.'

'You're being really kind, but I still feel useless. I couldn't even give you any money to help with the food.'

Lucinda shakes her head. 'When you find a true friend, you know the joy they bring to you. You don't always see the joy you bring to them. You, in that hostel, cradling Shannon in your arms to settle her; all the weight of the World on your shoulders, and you carry it! For her sake, you carry it all! You're an inspiration to me; a shining light, a star in the darkness.'

'Thank you,' Lianne says, with a few gentle tears. 'Thanks, sis!' and they hug each other.

Together, they carry the travel cot upstairs to the spare bedroom, Shannon still sleeping peacefully in it.

'I'll probably be gone when you wake up,' Lucinda says. 'See you tomorrow evening.'

Lianne nods, worn out from the day's events and also from crying. 'Night, then...'

'Sweet dreams.' Lucinda closes the door.

Settling down into the comfortable bed, Lianne realises that her weariness feels different to usual. Tonight it's a good tiredness. She needed to cry, needed to think about things, needed a lifeline. And Shannon and Lucinda together have pulled her from utter despair. No candle by her bed tonight, but she feels a light is burning bright in her heart. She gladly settles into sleep, wondering what strange dreams might come to her after a day unlike any she has lived through before.

Lucinda is with her father, walking through a vast hallway. The brightness on their faces comes from a multitude of small, flickering flames which fill the air around them.

'How goes the work?' he asks, as if he doesn't know.

'There's nothing like it,' she replies, smiling, 'stepping into the World and bringing the light to children's eyes. And they're all children, lost in a dark night. Like the widow, Saorse. The cold would have taken her if I hadn't placed the candle in her window.'

'Yes,' he replies, the joy of memory dancing in his eyes, 'she was so happy to see you again after all those years! Instead of fear and sorrow, there was a smile on her face when she closed her eyes months later on a bright summer's day, and tears of delight when she opened them to endless light.'

'Remember Novice Elspet who was starting to doubt her calling? All of those precious women; it was such a joy to be their abbess for a season.'

'She became abbess herself, you know, twenty years after you left; she kept the light burning strong in that place. So many mouths were fed and lives saved through her humility.'

'And Penny, whose friends lied to her, saying they would meet up, just so they could laugh at her for falling for their trick.'

'She found a better friend in you that evening.'

Lucinda looks around at some of the lights which are guttering or barely burning. 'So many lost in the darkness of their lives... so distant and cold.'

'Until you wake the light, breathe on the embers, tend the flame.'

'All those who let me,' she says, with sorrow for those who walk away instead. The father nods sadly; his heart, too, is broken for them.

Every light around them is precious. They are not isolated, but connected, weaving around each other in a tapestry of bright filigree. Two of the lights in particular catch their attention, woven tightly together as they dance; a young mother and her baby daughter, shining ever brighter as both start to see that the World's darkness cannot overcome them, for they are each other's light.

LIGHT REVOLUTION

J B WISKEY

Friday

The Sun was vivid and unique that Friday. It seemed to have changed colour. How long do they say it takes sunlight to travel to our Earth? A little more than eight minutes. Not long.

Saturday

'Mother, it's Floyd. I'm upstairs.'

There was stillness and a trembling loss of patience manifesting itself in the hallway. 'I can't keep calling you Floyd, Tony. This is just getting too much for my nerves. I didn't marry Floyd. You never told me about Floyd while we were engaged. You certainly didn't mention anything about the dressing up and role-play that...' there was exasperated hesitation blended with a soft rising anger, '... that our perfect marriage would consist of.'

Now there was stillness and a calculated silence from upstairs.

Or was there?

The house was so bereft of noise that Sally could not be sure Tony *was* actually upstairs anymore – that maybe, with her final naming of this bizarre behaviour of his, he had disappeared, drawn back in a nanosecond to the other dimension he had undoubtedly arrived from fifteen years previously. She looked up through the bannisters, straining to notice any atmospheric disturbance; any wormholes that might have conveniently opened and deported Tony back to his original cosmos. No clues struck her retina, no stirring of fifth-dimensional activity echoed towards her eardrums.

She sighed.

Taking off her absurdly heavy shoes so as to be as quiet as possible in her ascent, she climbed the straw-coloured carpeted stairs. She thought of taking her costume off as she went, as a gesture of the finality of her part in his game, but he'd helped her get into it all and she'd need his help or some scissors to get out. Scissors! Yes. She would use scissors to get out.

As she rounded the corner up the last steps, there he was, in his costume, stock-still. His make-up running a bit in the heat, his face poking out. He gave a pitiful whinny and pawed the ground as he saw her.

'Oh, Tony,' she murmured, some gentle love creeping back in against her will, 'you do make a wonderful-looking foal, but I'm just never going to feel comfortable dressed as a horse.'

Floyd looked momentarily confused. This was not how Mother of Floyd usually spoke to him, and Sally realised that in his costume, he had not clearly heard what she had called out from the hall. He'd just caught the tone of her voice and had waited with some trepidation to find out the new turn their long-running horseplay would take. He removed his head, mopped his brow with his fetlock, then helped Sally take hers off too.

Tony worked at the Cambridge Equine Hospital to the west of the city, and though he'd insisted on many occasions that he had developed the Floyd scenario specifically to be emotionally supportive of Sally, once they'd found out conclusively that she could not have children, Sally herself was pretty clear that Floyd had been kicking around inside Tony for much longer than Tony had been kicking around inside Floyd.

Sally repeated what she had called up from the hallway and Tony, quickly gauging the new position, suggested they take off their bridle wear, skip the groom and have a cup of tea. So they trotted downstairs to the kitchen. Tony had always been very active in talking things through and now was no different, tense though the situation might appear. It made Sally wonder why she had ignored her discomfort for so long and let the pressure build up inside her to such an extent, until she realised that in Tony's usual, clever way, he had deftly and playfully got her to put the bit between her teeth again, and was starting to sound very Floydy.

She went to the kitchen drawer next to the cooker, pulled the heavy-duty scissors out from the ordered assortment of implements, and cut straight through the throatlatch, the nose band and both cheek pieces of Mother of Floyd's Cavesson bridle.

'No, No, NO! Never again, Tony. The game is over.'

Tony watched Sally impassively while she continued with the scissors. With some care she ran them down the length of her costume from the neck to her left ankle, after which she shrugged off and stepped out of her horse hide for the last time. She gently replaced the scissors, shut the drawer and strode barefoot to the bathroom in nothing but her knickers and her horse make-up.

After mellowing out in the candlelit, sumptuously scented heat of the bath for a couple of hours, Sally cautiously emerged mid-evening to find that Tony had voluntarily decamped to the sitting room, and was watching *The Horse Whisperer* from underneath the spare duvet on the opened new sofa bed. She made toast and hummus for herself in a kitchen devoid of all evidence of the earlier horse flaying, took it to the bedroom with a cup of tea, and listened absently to the radio until sleep finally arrived.

Sunday

Since waking up, Sally had felt an urgent desire to escape, so had headed off to London. She'd come to the British Museum to a storytelling event that a colleague's husband had told her about. A retelling of the *Epic of Gilgamesh*, which turned out to be the oldest known written creation story, originating in Mesopotamian times – at least in its clay tablet state – with cuneiform script. The man with crow feathers in his hat, at the door to the BP Lecture Theatre, had told her in the interval that it would probably have been known and told through the oral tradition for hundreds or possibly thousands of years before the original written version, which itself was over 4,000 years old.

This idea and the spoken tale itself had begun to set her thoughts dancing to an unfamiliar tune. Crow-feather man had also told her that the passing on of the story, in the oral tradition, had continued through the millennia despite the written version on the clay tablets being lost to human eyes until early in 1850, when most of the tablets were excavated at the site of ancient Nineveh and translated. The astonishing thing was that the rhyming couplets used to tell the story by the traditional storytellers of the region at the time, the ashokhs, matched almost exactly with the cuneiform record that had lain hidden for a couple of thousand years in the earth. A story could be kept faithfully intact through a hundred generations.

The whole aim of Sally's Sunday getaway had been to leave behind every regularised pattern of her normal life and, free from Tony's presence, do something new and fresh to allow the depths of her inner workings some space to ruminate unhindered. Once she had plucked the memory of the 'performance storytelling', as Beatrice's husband had referred to it, from her 'Things I Must Forget' memory file, she had checked both performance and train times hastily, and fled from Floyd.

After the storytelling was over, she had found the ladies' toilets closed for repairs and as she was really desperate, had dived into the gents, which fortunately turned out to be empty of any gentlemen. There was just one cubicle. She went in and locked the door. For some reason she hadn't imagined the men's toilets could be kept as clean as the women's facilities, despite living with a fastidious, house-proud horse for so long. But so they were. She promptly lowered herself onto the seat and begun to go about her business.

Now, a great many things could have distracted her from making the momentous discovery she found herself sitting in front of, but as it went, a great many things had colluded over the previous twenty-four hours to bring Sally directly to her globally disruptive find.

Even in such relatively refined surroundings as these, she still noted there was graffiti to read. What was unexpected, though, was the quality of the read. And the length! Indeed, she only realised she must have been reading for more than half an hour when she heard the door to the toilets open and a guard call out, 'The museum will be closing in fifteen minutes.'

What she had found in this extraordinary piece of writing, which went neatly across two walls and the inside of the cubicle door, was not just engrossing and engaging, but truly revolutionary in its essence. Despite being a leading astrophysicist and having spent nearly two decades forging new inroads into quantum field theory and the density matrix, she had never read anything like this. It explained everything. Not just everything in her rarefied area of study, but everything she had ever had any question about.

A thirty-minute read had explained the functioning of the whole universe. The origins of organic life, what had been before the universe began, where we as a microcosmic particle of the incomprehensible whole were still heading and, most importantly, why.

And now, because the museum was about to close, she had to leave her tiny esoteric library and its only extraordinary book.

Although she had a good memory it was far from photographic, and every word of the graffiti treatise gave rich, integral nuance to the meaning of the whole. It was word-for-word perfection. But she'd come out without her phone because she had needed a proper break from Tony. She had needed a complete break from Floyd.

She could suddenly see, as her thoughts skipped back to the performance, that the toilet tract was even helping her make metaphysical and cosmological sense of the story of Gilgamesh, that this ancient tale wasn't just some made-up fiction but a set of complex psychological truths conveyed through story. And concurrently she saw that in fact, this chronicle of creation was helping her make sense of the cosmologically astonishing facts she had just read. Each vouched for the integrity of the other's account.

None of that helped her right now though to preserve the precious document in front of her. She would just have to come back here first thing in the morning to photograph it.

With her clear plan of intention now set in her mind,

she flushed the toilet and washed her hands, only to find that the hand dryer wasn't working and there was no hand-towel dispenser. She patted her hands, backs and palms, on the skirt of her dress, put on her coat, checked her reflection in the mirror and left the men's toilets. She walked purposefully out of the museum through the rear exit below the Joseph Hotung Gallery and into the dark, brisk evening. Autumn always gave her some inner warmth, despite most other people's mechanical complaints about 'this dreadful weather!' Occasionally she would retort to such petty moaning that 'the weather is just the weather, neither good nor bad, it's only our lack of appropriate clothing and our own attitudes that are dreadful'.

As this thought played out, and memories of many such dreadful attitudes ran through her head and got lodged there, she wondered if her own attitude towards Floyd was simply that too. Was she just wearing inappropriate clothing for the situation? Well, no. The Floyd situation called for exactly the clothing Tony had made for each of them. So her attitude then? That was indeed a problem. She certainly suffered from the attitude she had towards Floyd, and now Tony was suffering from it too. However – she had NOT signed up for Floyd or her own guise as Mother of Floyd. And hell, why didn't Mother of Floyd have her own name?

By now she had walked from the museum to King's Cross station and was boarding a fast train back to Cambridge. As she sat thinking and the train slipped away from the urban glow and into the velvet blackness of night, she pushed aside the circle of Floyd thoughts and came back to the cosmic teachings of the cubicle. She desperately wanted to write down all she could recall of the revelatory chirography, but in her haste that morning, and very uncharacteristically, she had also left the house without pen and paper.

Her mind often offered her thoughts and conundrums that needed to be noted down as her thinking continued to motor on, such as how composite targets and range equations are influenced in scattering theory, but this day, this most vital of all days, she had been too keen to change her daily routine, and this particularly useful habit had also fallen by the way because of that decision.

If there had been any expectations about the storytelling, they were that she could have a couple of hours of being lost, mindlessly in a fairy tale; of not having to think of her shabby and possibly catastrophic personal life. This had been the case in a way, but in fact the depth and profundity of the tale of Gilgamesh and his adopted brother, Enkidu, the power and imagery that the storyteller had so skilfully seeded in her unwittingly fecund imagination, were such that something in her own inner world had been found, while at the same time her mundane life's problems had receded into the countryside of the land of Lostness.

When she arrived home and walked through the front door, to her great relief she found a note from Tony that read: *Hay! Not feeling very stable - sleeping under the stars tonight. Floyd. X.* She smiled and went through to the study to write down some notes from the Toilet Tract. Somewhat distressingly, all she could remember now was something about '... the presumptions of any assumptions cannot lead to the reality of any verifiable Truth. Look well upon every foundation anew.'

Slightly alarmed, Sally paced round the room fervently rummaging about in her brain for some other parts of the extraordinary whole which had altered the course of her life. She now started to doubt her mind's capacity to be faithful, and the day's voyage into unfamiliar realms seemed ever more dreamlike. Had it really happened? The whole episode had that air of the surreal that only something so out of one's known experience can suddenly draw into one's conscious thinking.

'Go to bed. Get some sleep,' she persuaded herself out loud. And she did.

Monday morning
As Monday suddenly arrived in Sally's consciousness, before she even lifted her eyelids to greet the day, she could not avoid the recollection of seismic shifts her world had been shaken by over the weekend. Her marriage to Tony could surely not survive much longer, at least not in the strange hippomanic form it had grown into over the last few years.

Her work life, by turn, was not going to suffer as much as get struck by a cataclysmic act of God. The meteorite shower that knocked her askew when Floyd was unsaddled had only been a warning sign of the great asteroid's direct strike: the toilet cubicle tract. It was an event whose influence could potentially radiate outwards so violently, like a tsunami of transcendental change, that most of the modus operandi of modern civilisation would likely fall apart.

The writing had been so clear in its form, so plain in what it said and so simple to grasp, that it didn't actually need an astrophysicist's brain to absorb and comprehend its fundamental meaning. Everyone would be changed. Everything would change. Okay, initially just people's thinking; their mental processes would be disrupted, but this level of gross synaptic reconfiguration throughout the entire populace would become manifest in people's behaviour very quickly. She could see it in her own attitudes already, less than a day after ingesting these few transmutational words herself.

On the train ride into London, Sally made a few calls to old, trusted colleagues who had all become respected heads of research at Imperial College, King's College or UCL, but nobody answered and she had to leave messages for all of them. She took a taxi from the station to the rear entrance of the museum where security queues were generally shorter and speedier, and hurried onward to her lavatory library.

As she turned the corner she now found one of those CAUTION WET FLOOR signs in front of the men's toilets and one on the door that read: TOILETS CLOSED FOR CLEANING AND MAINTENANCE – the exact same notices that she had found at the entrance to the ladies the day before. Her heart beat faster at the thought that those precious words might have been unknowingly and carelessly washed away. She gently pushed the door open, went through the inner door and found a uniformed cleaner between herself and the final door she hoped to pass through.

'I'm desperate for the toilet, can I get past, please?' she lied.

He stood, propped on his mop, and looked unexpectedly hard and deep into Sally's eyes. 'As the ladies' room is just down the corridor, I suspect that is not the real question you want to ask me.'

Face to face with this man's firm gaze, Sally became unsure of herself, and she momentarily faltered on her chosen path.

'If you can't ask the right question,' he continued philosophically, in his unhurried East End accent, 'how can you hope to find the right answer?'

Recollecting herself, she cautiously came clean to the cleaner. 'Is... the writing in the cubicle still there?'

The man remained still, with a question running through his own mind, assessing the woman in front of him and her possible motives. Sally was trying to work out if there was an even more direct way to ask him, and just as she was ready to be more assertive, he spoke in his considered manner.

'I have not yet washed my words away.'

'I'd like to photograph *your* words,' she replied slowly, mimicking his tone somewhat.

'Go ahead.' He stepped towards the sinks and carried on his work as if their exchange had not happened.

Sally pushed open the cubicle door and went in. The toilet seat lid was closed and she sat down, folding her coat on her lap. The seated position offered the best angle to photograph the writings, which were indeed intact. She took out her phone, unlocked it and tapped the camera icon. The first shot still had the flash on and the writing was mostly lost in the reflected glare. She switched it off and started again. It took a dozen shots to capture the whole tract, and she checked each shot meticulously for clarity until she knew for certain she had the complete work. She tried to email it to herself for extra security, but there was no signal down in the subterranean depths of the museum. As she stood up, she automatically flushed the loo and washed her hands, as her contemplation about what she had photographed took precedence over her actions. The hand dryer still wasn't working and there was still no hand-towel dispenser. She patted her hands, backs and palms, on the seat of her trousers, grabbed her coat and left the small room.

Outside, the man continued working attentively.

'Did you say "my" words?' she asked.

He didn't look up. 'I did.'

'Are you the graffiti writer and the cleaner of graffiti too?' she posited. 'Where are these ideas from?'

He continued his scrubbing. 'No. I'm not the author.' Although he hadn't written them, he felt protective and a certain ownership of the words he had been the first to read. Then he straightened up and turned to face Sally once more. 'Are these ideas familiar to you?'

Sally's attention was distracted for a second by the security pass hanging on the lanyard round his neck, which had previously been hidden. The name read 'A Floyd'.

'No, they aren't. Except I read them yesterday evening. I had to use this toilet as the ladies was off limits for... cleaning.'

In a changed tone, A Floyd said, 'I have to finish up here. Perhaps we could meet for coffee in an hour and talk?'

'Err, yes. Yes, let's meet. Where?'

'At the bottom of the stairs outside here. We can go to the staff canteen; the coffee's better and much cheaper, and it'll be considerably quieter than the courtyard. Eleven thirty?'

Sally nodded and left the men's toilets.

She wanted desperately to be talking to A Floyd right now, but instead she went upstairs to the Great Court and walked its marble floors as she pondered.

A text came through on her phone: *We should talk this evening. Floyd.* It took a moment to reframe and realise that this was a text from Tony, not A Floyd. She didn't reply.

A moment later, a call came through from an Imperial College friend, an evolutionary biologist with an interest in theories that ranged far beyond what he taught within his tired Darwinist remit. Tazeem was privately writing a groundbreaking theory that he had discussed with Sally on numerous occasions during the years they'd known each other, as he and a growing number of colleagues in his discipline acknowledged the untenable nature of a large proportion of Darwin's interesting but flawed theory.

'Sally? What's going on? Where are you?'

'I'm in the British Museum and there's something here you have to see. Now.'

Without hesitation Tazeem responded, 'I can be there in a couple of hours, but I've got a hundred and twenty "eager" students waiting for my massively exciting lecture on cavity-nesting bees and wasps starting in... less than twenty minutes. I can get to you by about one o'clock, will that do? What's it all about?'

'That'll be fine, Tazeem. Yes. Fine. Yes. Listen. It's a strange situation, it's utterly bizarre, but I've found some writing that has thrown light on... well, let's say it looks like you've been right about where your own ideas have been taking you. You know, the fossil record that shows a distinct lack of any gradual change and everything that that implies. You were really onto something when you talked about light and its effects through the cosmos, but this piece of writing, the tract I've read, it's new and... God, there's so much that my head's going crazy with it, but it's comprehensive, cohesive and I think answers everything, at least all the sciences I know anything about. It's not just about evolution. You know, I don't think we can refer to evolution as evolution anymore actually – but you need to read it yourself. Do you think you could find Chinedu and get him to come along too? I did leave him a message.'

'I can try. God knows what kind of lecture I'm going to be able to pull together after all you've just told me, but yup, I'll find Chin and meet you – where exactly?'

'Outside the BP Lecture Theatre downstairs.'

'Okay, I know it. 1 p.m.' Tazeem hung up and Sally continued her walk.

During the next thirty minutes two other colleagues called her back; one who taught physics at King's and the other an astrophysicist at UCL who hinted that he had something pretty massive to share with her too. 'Before it gets out to the press, though things are already being noticed,' he had said enigmatically.

At the appointed time, Sally was at the bottom of the stairs by the lecture theatre as A Floyd came towards her proffering a hand to shake. 'Arthur. Arthur Floyd. Reluctant cleaner of graffiti.'

'Sally Hammerton, accidental reader of graffiti,' she replied playfully.

As Arthur led Sally through STAFF ONLY and along corridors with endless foil-lagged heating pipes, through more doors and up a lift to another corridor, he related his part of the story: One of the department curators had found the graffiti in the gents on Friday, and without reading it, Arthur had to assume, and finding the hand dryer broken as well, he had ordered the service desk to get a handyman on the job. Arthur was sent and, routinely checking the ladies too, had found similar writing there. It seemed to him to be in a different hand, but he had read and photographed it before reluctantly cleaning it off on Sunday afternoon. When the museum had closed, he'd visited as many loos as he could in the sprawling building to check for more writing, but had found nothing further.

Arthur was in his early fifties and had led an exceptionally unexceptional existence, just plodding through life, married most happily to Gigi with two grown kids and a grandchild on the way. He'd had a few long-running menial jobs that had helped see to his family's upkeep, and that was enough for him. Their wellbeing and growth was the focus of his life. He wasn't ambitious and had never looked much deeper at the world around him until the previous couple of days, which had expanded his perception so vastly and with such velocity that he had thought his head and chest were going to explode. Once he'd taken measure of her, Sally's arrival had been a great relief. He hadn't known what to do with the writings while they were busy doing so much within him.

'Here we are.' He held open the canteen door for Sally. 'Grab something to eat too if you like, my treat. I'm going to have my lunch now; I got in at seven this morning and didn't take my tea break.'

Sally wasn't that hungry, so just got a pastry with her coffee. As they sat down away from other people, Arthur confided, 'I'm so glad to have someone to talk to about it. I love Gigi, but I couldn't bring her here today and you have to read it to get it, don't you think?' Sally nodded her agreement, and as Arthur tucked into his lasagne, Sally told him her story. He was even more reassured now to hear that she was a serious scientist, and that what was blowing his mind actually was genuine mind-blowing material, even for a professor. That this wasn't something that most other people would already know about, and he was right to be in awe of it.

He almost shed a tear as he thought about having destroyed the writing in the ladies' loo, but he had been on the case enough to photograph it all, and now he swiftly brought up the photos on his phone for Sally to look at. She read a little, recognising the same quality and integrity in the writing, but as Arthur had said, it was clearly written by another hand, though maybe with the same pen.

'I won't read it all now, Arthur. Can you send it to me?'

They exchanged emails and numbers, and he sent her the precious images.

As they both silently held their own thoughts for a moment, Arthur began to look serious, then concerned. 'Sally, what do I do? Do I clean the men's graffiti as well?'

'No no no. This is too important. I've already made some calls, and four other scientists are on their way here for one o'clock. Can you lock the cubicle so that only you have access? Say that you're waiting for a spare part, that the sink's blocked or the lock doesn't work. Whatever it takes.'

'Yes, I can do that.' He physically relaxed and his face brightened.

Sally now took control. 'Good. Once my colleagues have read it and can verify I'm not dreaming all this, then we can go to the museum director and have it closed off officially, get more specialists in to read it, and really get working.'

Arthur was feeling quite out of his depth, though he sensed the reality of what was happening. He knew his small part in this major world event was almost fulfilled and he spoke up. 'I want Gigi to come to see it too. For herself. Before it gets lost to us mere mortals.'

'Yes, good. Good idea, Arthur. Call her, get her here right now. This is all going to move very quickly.' A shiver of entwined emotions sped through Sally's body. It hadn't even occurred to her to share this with Tony, the man she had once upon a time wished to share everything of value with.

Arthur stopped eating his pudding to call his beloved Gigi.

'Gigi... I know you are, luv, but look, you just have to forget work today. I need you to come to the museum. Now. And get Billy and Diana to come with you... yes... yes... I'm very serious... no... no... it's nothing bad, luv. But it really is really important. I can't make more calls right now, just tell the kids to drop everything. It's something wonderful and special, but it has to be now, okay? Right now. Come to the Lecture Theatre... yes, where the storytelling was last month... yes... I love you too.'

Sally rang her not-so-beloved-just-now gee-gee. She shared her news and asked him to come. Tony didn't sound surprised to hear Sally's request, and agreed to leave work straight away, gallop to the station and jump on a train. He would be there by about three o'clock.

Monday afternoon

Less than an hour after Arthur had spoken to her, Gigi arrived with their daughter Diana, who was seven months pregnant and already waddling with the magnificent scale of her tummy. After meeting Sally and being briefed as to why they were there, the two ladies were surreptitiously guided into the gents and to the little library. As Sally left to wait for her fellow scientists, the door was closed and Diana with her gravid belly took the only seat, Gigi squatting beside her, and they commenced their reading.

At first in the cubicle there was some giggling at the odd situation the women found themselves in on that unusual Monday. Then as time passed some murmuring was audible to Arthur, waiting outside, as the two of them explained some parts to each other and discussed others.

In a short while all four scientists had arrived, and, with Sally, quietly filed into the men's room to join Arthur. As they stood lingering, the gathered ensemble heard a few small gasps from inside the cubicle and finally a loud 'Dear God, Arthur! Is all this real?' from Gigi. 'Does it really mean that...?' She was unable to even finish her question as she realised she knew the answer. She knew so much now. With that, Diana and Gigi came out, looking quite stunned. Their universe had been infinitely expanded.

As well as their devoted Arthur, and Sally the scientist, there were now three more men and a woman who hadn't been there when they went in. Arthur ushered his loved ones to one side and held them both tightly to him.

While the distinguished new arrivals had waited, they had been gently amused by the sounds coming from inside the toilet. But now they saw these two ordinary women emerge, who had obviously undergone something truly powerful, and they couldn't wait to go to the toilet themselves and start reading. It was quite an awkward squeeze to have four people in the cubicle, while still allowing enough space to read the walls. Francine, the physicist from King's, was offered the seat by the gents in the gents, and reading began in earnest.

Sally waited with a mixture of nervousness and exhilaration, as if it were her own work that her esteemed colleagues were scrutinising.

When Arthur took his womenfolk out from the toilets, they found Billy loitering by the lecture theatre doors, still oblivious to why he had been summoned. After his immediate concerns at the strange state he found his mother and pregnant sister in were calmed, Billy waited eagerly for his turn to read the world-changing script.

As the excited scientists exited, Billy and Arthur went in.

Carlos, a prominent astrophysicist originally from Mexico, was speaking. 'It all fits with what we've been finding over the weekend. Everyone's noticed the sun, how it seems different, yes?' They all nodded. 'Well, it is. On Friday it changed, and I don't mean in any recognised way such as sunspots, solar flares or coronal mass ejections. The sun changed.'

Carlos stopped while they all tried to assimilate his statement. Relating it to what they had just been reading, it made perfect sense, but that something this vast had actually happened and they weren't in a sci-fi movie – that needed a moment to permeate their minds and their hearts.

To have read The Tract, which itself fine-tuned or reconfigured all scientific theory, which gave answers to the questions that each of them had been driven by since their own scientific awakenings years before, was something extraordinary, mind-altering and magnificent, despite the unfamiliar and disturbing background odour of unforeseeable consequences that would undoubtedly come. But now. Now the sun had changed!

Carlos went on to answer the initial question of 'How has it changed?' that everyone was too stunned to give voice to, which hung in the air like a pregnant herd of gravity-defying elephants. 'Sunlight is faster than it was before. Considerably faster. And...' he hesitated to say what he could still barely comprehend himself, 'there is a new colour. The spectrum of natural sunlight holds a new visible colour unlike any of the known colours, visible or invisible. A new colour I have no words to describe.'

By the time Tony arrived, just before three o'clock, Billy had surfaced from the loo on wobbly legs with wondrous tears running down his cheeks, and a number of other scientists were on their way.

Sally escorted Tony in and stood beside him while he sat and read. After a few minutes he reached up and held Sally's hand firmly, saying, as if talking to himself, 'Ah yes. Good.' When he was done, he stayed very still. 'I'm so glad it was you who found this. It's so fitting.'

Sally smiled quietly and her heart was content.

'And the writing in the ladies' toilets?' he asked.

'Mr *Floyd*,' she emphasised the name, 'the maintenance man, washed it off yesterday while I was in here discovering this part. He did photograph it before erasing it though.'

'That's good,' said Tony, who had grinned broadly on hearing the maintenance man's name. 'It's all very good.'

As the Hammertons emerged, the second influx of scientists had begun to appear, and now they commenced their orderly viewing process. Sally caught Arthur's eye and beckoned him over to introduce her husband to the preserver of The Tracts. As the two Floyds shook hands, she said to Arthur, 'It's time for me to see your superiors and let them know there is an urgent historical event happening in their toilet.'

Once Arthur had made some calls on the internal phone system, Sally and Carlos had gone to meet the museum director, Mr Fischer, in his office, and during their conversation a detached question floated across the sea of Sally's thoughts: how did Tony know there was writing in the ladies' toilets too? But this question was soon out of Sally's immediate sight and over the horizon, as she was swept along with Mr Fischer's gathering of his considerable focused energies, to fully engage with the unprecedented situation she had brought to his door.

Tuesday
Headlines in the world's press reported that across Northern Europe and in parts of Asia, the colour of grass had changed.

Saturday, seven months later, at home
Sally stopped her intense writing and raised her head to see Tony as he came into her study and stood in front of the desk.

He looked very sheepish, even though he was dressed as a horse.

Sally wasn't surprised. She'd been noticing plenty of pre-Floyd signs in Tony's behaviour over the past week. He was holding a dandy brush for grooming and over his arms there was the skin of Mother of Floyd, which he had made whole once more through a long, secret process of painstakingly hand-stitching it back into its original, wearable form...

Everywhere else, that same Saturday

The world was transforming all around them in ways that nobody could have predicted, neither Nostradamus nor any fiction writer of the twenty-first century, let alone the futures analysts and traders in the City, whose jobs no longer existed.

The fervent unrest, the enormous protests and the initial clashes with riot police and military forces all around the world, which had resulted in many deaths, had dissolved after a few weeks of horrible conflict. Soldiers, uniformed police officers and angry young men and women with bricks, staves and Molotov cocktails in their fierce hands, had all lowered their weapons, their shields and their masks, and sat down in the streets to start talking about the content of The Tracts. In time they had helped each other put out recently started fires, they had set overturned vehicles back on their wheels, and generally tidied things up.

McDonald's was preparing to reopen more than thirty thousand restaurants to exclusively serve organic, vegan, slow food and fresh juices.

Petrol sales had almost stopped, of course, and the oil industry all but ceased to operate. The majority of petrol station forecourts, with their idle, empty pumps standing silent, had become makeshift Conversion Houses, where those with an aptitude for it worked tirelessly and joyfully each day, transforming vehicles by replacing the obsolete combustion engines with new engines that ran on compressed air, or sealed motors that ran on pure water and didn't pollute or need refuelling because the water was continually recycled within the unit. There was so much revolutionary technology just waiting in the wings to burst forth and fill the voids left by the dearly departed, anachronistic machinery.

The Tracts had appeared all over the world at the same time, in many languages, written in many hands, using a multitude of different writing implements. No one had ever claimed authorship of any of them. Though some talked of The World Brotherhood of New Light, a mysterious collective of metanoiic thinkers spread out across the globe, who had been talking about just such a transformational cosmic occurrence for decades, nobody had taken much notice of them then, and nobody knew who they were now. Any organisation of this kind that might once have been, had since quietly ceased to be.

There were radio and TV channels across the globe now dedicated exclusively to the continuous broadcasting of The Tracts, but most of the time people still gathered each day, as they had done at the beginning, at what had become known as their local Reading Houses, to hear The Tracts read out loud and to discuss... all and everything there was to discuss: life, their now-beloved planet Earth and the endless universe.

Plenty of the world's other familiar old institutions had changed beyond recognition, or had just quietly come to an end altogether.

Every grocery, from the largest supermarket to the smallest corner shop, was filled with a wildly different array of fare than there had been BT (Before Tracts). There was very little processing of farm produce anymore; everything was organic (or 'food' as it had been called a century before), and there was no need for warning labels, as organophosphates, glyphosate and other toxic chemicals were finally accepted as being unnecessary for food production, as well as damaging to the health of people, animals and the environment, and were no longer used. There was zero plastic packaging.

Naturally, banks didn't exist nowadays, and all the old forms of government were being swept aside in their redundancy.

Schools? Well, old school buildings everywhere had become Learning Houses. People of all ages went to the Learning Houses whenever they wanted. To play, to nurture enthusiasm (which is easy when you're playing), and to follow the rhythms of their innate wish to explore and learn. There were no examinations, no qualifications, no hierarchy of achievements. What there was, was a great sense of open enquiry in which everyone participated.

And everybody grew on their own, original path.

There were Story Houses where Gilgamesh and other creation stories were told; where epics, myths, wonder tales and folk tales brought all kinds of people together; where each listener's emotions were exercised and exorcised; where another part of each human blossomed spontaneously. The Tract Story in any one of its local guises would be told, and like all stories set in the masterfully quarried stone of Truth, it was ever fresh and never tired of being heard.

After all the wars petered out, there was mass migration.

A great many people yearn in their hearts for the land of their forebears, and now, they could respond to this yearning. Traditional homelands were recognised and graciously reoccupied and shared peaceably, with a great deal of time and energy being given to slowly building new homes, new villages and entire cities, for the new time that had come. Buildings were being constructed in both the new way, with new means and materials, and in the old local traditional ways, using ancient means and materials, each system learning from the other.

There was a staggering amount of unemployment, as it would formerly have been called, but people didn't spend much time worrying about that. After all, there was an endless abundance of things for people to occupy themselves with, in this climate of radical change and extreme understanding. So if anyone needed feeding, clothing, housing or anything else, then their needs were met, because the idea that they were are all part of one whole, all cells of one unified body sharing a common purpose, was no longer just an idea, but a living reality. People began to *feel* and *know* it as fact, not just an empty expression used in their everyday dealings with each other.

A particularly powerful symptom of the arrival of this epoch, was what happened to the many hundreds of millions of people across the planet, who had been living with what were previously referred to as lifelong or terminal illnesses. They began to regain balanced health while their ailments receded, and over time completely disappeared. The change of diet and everybody having access to clean, living water sources were obvious causes in many cases of regenerative health, but the most compelling and transformative healing was due to the new light. By spending more time in sunlight rather than under the glare of artificial light, and no longer blocking the sun's pure nourishment with old-fashioned sunscreens, and by eating the appropriate foods and microalgae, people experienced almost immediate alleviation from all diseases. Those who spent time looking at the New Rainbows or watching the sun rise, were those who healed quickest.

Rainbows, with their new eighth colour, had been the single most impressive change in the first days of The Tracts. The mainstream media agencies had gone crazy with it all, even though neither screen nor print technology could register the new colour. New Rainbows weren't simply tagged on as feel-good articles at the end of the main news, with its regular stream of fear, hate and corporate advertising disguised as news. No. Rainbows made headlines every day. At least for the couple of weeks before the old mogulised media system collapsed.

The New Rainbow phenomenon had given scientists a place at the forefront of the changes, especially those close to The Tracts and those who were directly discovering what extraordinary transformations were afoot in the universe, and on our modest but meaningful little planet. And for the time that these phenomena were in the limelight, scientists were also in the media's glare as their expertise was called upon to bring rigorous clarity for the initially concerned population.

Scientists of every stripe turned their attention to the global crisis, to understanding the consequences of the Sun's amplified speed and more radiant emissions. Everybody was under the influence of the sun. The Tracts helped astronomers permeate the mysteries of dark matter so thoroughly that it became clear in the light of all the newly unfolding evidence that neither cold nor warm dark matter actually existed. It had become an unnecessary theoretical filling-in of a gap that was no longer there to be filled. The Tracts' unified theory of everything was relatively quickly and conclusively proven to be true, as the quantum and macroscopic laws that allow the universe to function were harmoniously married, and the two became one.

Breakthroughs were witnessed daily, often hourly, in all fields, as entrenched scientific dogma fell away under the influence of The Tracts.

Science was erupting.

Mankind was erupting.

Three and a half years after the Sun's metamorphosis, the light from Earth's nearest and dearest stars would begin to arrive in a similarly altered state. The three stars that make up Alpha Centauri would be first, and they would demonstrate that they had undergone the very same transition at the exact same time as our own modest star, which was all calculated in accordance with the new speed of light. Their light would be found to hold the new spectrum too. As the light from each star arrived in the ensuing years, and saturated everything, it would continue to bring more profound and subtle shifts for organic and human life on Mother Earth.

Something had affected all the stars in our galaxy, and possibly the whole universe, at the same time. An instantaneous, galaxy-wide occurrence that relegated visible light, even with its increased velocity, to the status of second-fastest thing in the universe. But now, we knew that. We all knew that. Virtually every person on Earth had read or heard The Tracts and continued to do so as their understanding grew deeper with experience. We all understood light, time, quantum gravity and energy. Everybody understood how they worked together and what their purpose was. With this whole learning process came a magnified aspiration that touched every soul to listen more seriously. This in turn had profound effects, realigning people's hearts to their true direction.

At home
As Sally stood up, got undressed and began, with Floyd's help, to wriggle inelegantly into her old equine skin, she calmly said, with the brightest and broadest of smiles, 'You know, my dear Tony-Floyd, you're going to have to make me a whole new outfit very soon!' Tony gave

her an inquisitive, cautious glance as he bent down to buckle her hooves on. In response to his look she simply announced; 'Mother of Floyd is with foal.'

In spite of how utterly infertile Sally had been BT, everything was different now. While the global birth rate was set to plummet as the number of new pregnancies dropped in every territory, by as much as two-thirds, ex-professor Sally Hammerton, part-time horse and reader of graffiti, was inconceivably pregnant.

THE CROWS

KATE ROY

The clocks are dead. The sky is a strange red colour and the moon is always full. I cannot see the city skyline. There doesn't appear to be anything beyond the university grounds. The lawn outside the campus doors is covered in crows. There is no grass. It is as if the lawn is made of the things: a seething, writhing, shrill, feathery black mass. I cannot get across the lawn to the entrance gates. I had tried to. The noise got too much for me. I tried to run across the heads of the birds to the gates on the other side. The crows did scatter but the lawn crumbled underneath my feet and I had to jump back through the front doors to avoid falling into the abyss. The crows flew back into the empty spaces, blocking them up. I'm almost entirely certain that the lawn is made up of pure crow now.

If I'm going to be trapped in a building with no discernible escape, I suppose I could do worse than my university building. I have books in the library and food in the canteen; more than enough to keep me alive. The shadows get to me though. I'd say there are roughly 400 people who go to my school. I now share the building with 400 shadows. They look like people but I can't make out their faces. They are merely shapes. I don't bother them and they don't bother me. I can't even touch them. I wonder if I am just a shadow to them.

It gets lonely with no one to talk to. I found an ancient ham radio in the basement but all I can get from it is muffled cries and the occasional Latin chorus. Some of the channels are just pure white noise. I like those the best. Most nights, I bring a bean-bag down from the library and try to fall asleep to the sound of white noise that never seems to quite drown out the chorus of the crows outside. All night long, they sing to their endless, silent red sky.

My name is Mark Greenwood. For the most part I'd lived a fairly typical life. Well. It depends what your definition of 'typical' is, but all in all I can't imagine my life sounds terribly unusual or exciting. I was a student attending university. I had a family, a girlfriend and, as far as I knew, a future. I was born on 13 June 1991. I was a pretty ugly baby but my parents loved me, as far as I could tell. Then, one day, I found myself trapped in a twisted version of my university with no idea as to how I got there. It was like waking up the next morning and being unable to remember the exact moment I fell asleep. No matter how hard I tried I couldn't remember the final memory I had from my old life.

The university campus is a large building. It has more than enough facilities to keep me alive and (in theory, at least) sane. The ground floor consists of a large cafeteria and a cluster of teachers' offices. There are several floors above it consisting mostly of classrooms, and a basement below that is mainly used for storage. There are two large tower blocks directly adjacent to the main building, flanking it on either side. The one on the left is mostly offices, classrooms and lecture halls. The one on the right is a massive library with a foyer on the ground floor and several floors of bookshelves and IT suites above it. This structure is surrounded on all sides by a lush, verdant lawn with wrought-iron gates enclosing it. Soon enough, those gates came to look like prison bars to me.

Despite the vastness of my domain, I was in such shock for the first couple of days that I was practically catatonic. Then I went slightly mad and rampaged through the halls desperately trying to find a way out. This was when I made my ill-fated escape attempt. I then tried to communicate with the shadows to no avail. Eventually I just settled into a routine of eating and sleeping, of simply getting through each day. After eight weeks, I realised I was getting complacent. I decided to stop feeling sorry for myself. I tried to think about things logically. If I couldn't get off the premises, then I should try to communicate with the outside world. The ham radio was no use. How else can you communicate over long distances? With a phone? No good – there wasn't mobile reception; I'd tried to use my phone before it died. I'd also tried all the landlines in the teachers' on-campus offices as well as the nurses' station. No good there, either. The Internet? I went to one of the IT suites and sat down at a computer. I fished my wallet out of my rucksack. With no mobile reception and no lectures to go to, my bag and its contents were virtually useless, but I was still loath to let it go. I don't know why. Maybe because it was the only thing that I had from my old life; back when I attended university in a world that wasn't crawling with ghostly figures and demonic birds. I took my student ID card out of my wallet and typed in my ID number and password. A box appeared on the screen with a harsh, mechanical sound: 'The ID you entered is not recognised by this system.' I tried several more times. Every time the harsh 'ping' that accompanied the error message on the screen seemed to be chastising me for even trying. The squawks and shrieks of the crows outside grew louder and louder. It felt as though they were mocking me. In my frustration, even the air seemed to hum like a swarm of angry bees. My temper was at breaking point. I wanted a good excuse to throw a tantrum so I typed my password one more time. The harsh ping and petulant little text box dutifully appeared on screen. I lifted up the computer, tearing the connector from its socket, and threw the machine across the room. It smashed against the wall to a chorus of shattering glass, crunching plastic and sparking wires. The thunderous noise broke some of the tension that had been building up inside me. I walked out of the suite and strode briskly down the hallway, dissipating ghostly figures as I went. I waited until I had locked myself in the supply cupboard before I allowed myself to cry. I don't know why I waited to find somewhere private. It was not as if anyone could see me.

So that was it. I was stuck under a red sky besieged by black crows. I fell into a deep depression. I had previously tried to maintain a routine: wake up at a certain time, go for a jog round the hallways, eat breakfast in the canteen, spend the morning scouting the building, stretch, have lunch, read in the library for an hour, stretch again... I liked stretching. The sharp feeling of strained muscles and the buzz of relief afterwards always calmed me down when things seemed to get on top of me. But after a while, those feelings just didn't have the same appeal to me and I found myself merely going through the motions. The sweet tang of food became bitter, the refreshing crispness of water became viscous and swamp-like and the gentle release of sleep became unsettling. Routine became less of a saving grace and more of a burden. The thought of having to do the same thing every day for an unknowable length of time sent me into a spiral of despair. I felt so empty. I would stay up all night until my eyes were raw and heavy and then spend the entire day trying to get back to sleep. Some days, it felt as though I had never woken up, or that something inside me refused to, and I wandered around the campus in a daze. On days when the frustration and anger filled my body and spilled out my mouth like sewage I would run around the hallways of the campus, not stopping until my muscles were raw and screaming and I couldn't take any more and I simply collapsed in a hallway. Or I would fling open a window and scream into the scarlet abyss until my cries mingled with those of the crows and my throat became red and raw. Some days, I would gather heavy objects I found in the classroom and toss them into the sea of birds. I would have given anything for a gun. I would have felt such huge delight in shooting down some of those black squawking bastards. But it was satisfying, nonetheless, to watch them shriek and scatter when one of my objects struck them with the force of a desk-chair or a copy of *War and Peace*. But then I would gaze down into the area they had vacated and see endless black space, and I would feel that black, empty feeling rise up within me again.

Now, I'm a modern man. I believe that people should be free to express their emotions without fear of ridicule. It is the twenty-first century after all. But I'm also just a stupid and frail man and to let anyone see me cry, to observe my naked despair and fear, would be just too vulnerable; too shameful. I don't know why it's so hard to admit to other people that you're alive. Only one person, apart from my family, has ever seen me cry and, at the time, I thought I would never see her again.

One day, I was curled up in the library, mumbling distractedly to myself. I couldn't quite register my surroundings because I was in such a stupor. But when I looked up at one of the shadows sitting beside me, I realised it was a girl because of the long hair floating about her head like cream in coffee and her plump bust resting on the desk in front of her. She was reading a book, turning the pages languidly with her head leaning on one hand. I missed girls. I missed their soft skin, their silken hair, the way their bodies moved in the velvety, secretive folds of their clothes. I missed the way they laughed melodically at foolishness and absurdity, the way they peered coquettishly from behind books. I missed the way they smelt of sweat and flowers, and the way they seemed able to personalise nearly anything with stickers and ribbons. I missed the pretty, ephemeral girls in short skirts and high heels who would walk past me on a cloud of air in hallways, eyes misted over by their glittery, ribbon-adorned dreams. But it wasn't only those girls I missed. I also missed the girls in shapeless black skirts with unshaven legs who sneered and snarled at everyone's exhausting baseness and stupidity in public and then went home and cried themselves to sleep. I missed girls who chopped their own hair off to piss off their parents; who flipped the bird behind the teacher's back and played with dead frogs when they were kids. But most of all, I missed Lucy. Lucy was all of those things and more. She was every shade of every heart. She was every girl who ever was and every woman who would ever be.

I didn't cry then. I don't think I had any tears left in me. I looked around the library and saw an air vent above a bookshelf. I shrugged. In my solitude, I'd debased myself in every possible manner. The only thing left was acts of utter absurdity. I walked over to the bookcase, clambered the shelves, scattering volumes of family law as I went, and crouched unsteadily beside the vent. After much struggling, I yanked it open and crawled inside. It was pitch black in there. I could barely see my hands in front of my face. It was icy cold and claustrophobic. And dirty; filled with clutter and debris. It was sticky and smelt of mould. It wasn't at all like the clean, spacious vents found in action movies that the hero has to clamber through to get the drop on vaguely Eastern European-sounding terrorists. I lay there for a while, feeling hollow and breathing in galaxies of dust. I thought about clambering through all the vents in the building, mapping them out and creating a system of passages. That might keep the loneliness and despair at bay for at least a little while. I tried crawling through the vent on my belly, but I was out of breath after only five minutes and pieces of sharp detritus kept poking me in my sides. I went limp with exhaustion and let my arms flop out in front of me. My fingers brushed against something rough but silky. My body stiffened. I scrambled forward and tentatively caressed the foreign object. I felt rough, hessian material and some kind of plastic buckle. It was the strap of a rucksack. I pulled on it and felt the heaviness of a full bag at the other end. Holding on to the strap, I wriggled out of the vent and lay exhausted on top of the bookshelf. I did cry then; tears of joy as I clutched that one sign of life that proved someone had been to this place other than me. I cried until I was empty. And then I passed out.

When I came to the first thing I did was feel for the rucksack. It was still there. I hadn't dreamt it. I clambered down the shelves clutching my precious cargo and, hands shaking, emptied the contents on a nearby table. There were several history books, a notepad, a congealed sandwich, a phone and a wallet. I opened the wallet and looked at the ID. It belonged to Joseph Pak: an English-Korean student who had been a 'smile and nod' friend of mine from history class. Near the beginning of the year, his bag had gone missing and he had been in quite a state about it. I had pretended to be concerned and half-heartedly helped him look for it before sneaking off to go be with Lucy. He ended up having to get everything in the bag replaced.

I skimmed through the books in the rucksack, imagining Joseph turning the pages. I read the notebook, trying to decipher Joe's unintelligible handwriting. He had drawn a lot of rabbits and naked women in the margins. I looked through his wallet, which contained £10 (not much use to me), an HMV loyalty card and some family photos. I glanced at the photos. There was Joseph as a kid looking awkward in a bow-tie posing stiffly next to his smiling parents; a laughing girl in a sundress on a beach who could be either a sister or a girlfriend; and Joseph smiling down at a fat baby sleeping in his arms. Even though I barely knew anything about Joseph Pak's life, family or personality, it felt as if I was rediscovering an old friend. I found myself wishing that I'd taken the time to get to know him.

I took the bag down to the basement that evening and went through the contents several times while the air crackled with white noise and the distant cries of the crows. I found it hard to sleep when night came. I lay awake for several hours staring at Joseph Pak's picture smiling blankly back at me from his ID card. I read his name, printed clearly below his smiling face, over and over again until the letters became meaningless shapes and swam in front of my eyes. I blinked a few times to clear my vision and found my eyes didn't want to open again.

I woke up some time later and rolled over, heaving a long sigh. I reached my arm out and felt the hard, shiny plastic of Joe's card. I looked at it for a long while. I felt hollow inside. The magic of it had worn off slightly with sleep and the prospect of spending an eternity with nothing but a smiling piece of plastic made me grumble darkly to myself. I languidly waved the card like a paper fan as I idly wondered what I should do with the rest of my day. But I couldn't think of anything I'd rather do than stare at Joseph's fixed laminate smile, even if it was kind of depressing. So I did. Then my eyes slipped to the student ID number below it. I stared at it, the gears in my head sluggishly moving towards a revelation. Could I use this ID to log into the computer system? It hadn't worked with my ID number. But my rucksack had come with me. This bag was already here. Maybe it would adhere to the internal logic of this place. Maybe it would work! Electrified by this idea, I hurried upstairs to the IT suite.

The computer I had thrown was still lying in a shattered heap against one wall. I sat down at another computer and, hands shaking, entered Joseph Pak's name and ID number. My body let out a breathless cry of joy as the university home screen appeared before my eyes. I did a little sitting-down, arm-flailing dance, something I hadn't done since I was a kid. I brought up email and tried sending an SOS to my parents, but a sad little message came up on screen when I clicked the 'send' button:

Sorry: you have no Internet connection.

I sighed deeply. I didn't feel angry or sad. There didn't seem to be much point. I explored the homepage for a while. Joseph had pretty good grades in history. Bs, mostly. I looked at the books he had taken out. As expected, they were mostly history textbooks. I scrolled down the page, looking over the titles half-heartedly. When I was near the bottom of the list, I saw a strange title sandwiched between a Napoleon biography and a book on the French Revolution. *Occultus: A Guide to Trans-dimensional Theory and Spell Book.* My brow furrowed. The surely academically minded Joseph Pak didn't seem to be the type to be interested in such hokum. I looked at the return date. He had returned it to the library just two days after he had taken it out. He must have borrowed it out of curiosity and then found it too spiritualist for his liking. But I was genuinely curious about this book. Lucy was a massive fan of witchcraft. She'd had loads of that kind of book at home.

I thought about Lucy while I wandered down to the main library foyer. She had lost many of her books in the move. Her parents had split up a couple of months before I came to this realm and it seemed as though Lucy had split apart as well. She seemed a different girl after her dad had buggered off to Manchester with his new lady. Last time I checked, she was fighting with her mum a lot and things were really tense at home. Lucy had lots of younger siblings and was often expected to look after them, making her really fed up with her new life. As a result she often sloped off to be with me instead, but for the last few weeks I had spent back in the real world I hadn't seen her as much. I found myself wishing that I could have seen her just once more before I was trapped here. That I could have held her and told her everything was going to be alright.

I clenched the rucksack tight in my hand and sighed raggedly. At least the hunt for this mysterious spell book would keep me occupied for a little while. I walked into the library foyer and checked for the book in the computer system. It was in the 'Spirituality and Religious Education' section on the top floor. There were several shadows on that floor, moving silently between the bookcases. But there were none in the Spirituality and RE section. I peered at the books. They all had indecipherable titles in other languages. Many of them appeared to be untranslated. The entire section was pretty neglected; the shelves were covered in dust and cobwebs. The far end of the shelves seemed to be part of some other world entirely. It was dim and unsettlingly quiet; a kind of oppressive, leaden silence. At least I could no longer hear the crows. I crouched down in the corner and sat there for a while, revelling in the silence. I retreated into myself, drifting in the space between sleep and waking.

Eventually, I grasped that I couldn't stay there forever, and that I had a mission to fulfil. I scoured the shelves at the back and, right at the bottom, found the book I was looking for. I heaved the large, heavy volume off the shelf and dragged it to a desk on the other side of the room.

I sat down to read it. It was in English, thankfully. According to the small slip of white paper taped in the front cover of the book, it had been taken out by only two people over the past five years. The first set of dates correlated with the information on Joseph Pak's homepage. Apparently, the person who had taken it out after him hadn't returned it yet. There was only a check-out date on the slip and no return date. Then what was it doing back in the library? The date it had last been taken out was marked down as being three weeks before I came to this dimension. I thought back. I hadn't seen Lucy a lot in those last three weeks. Were the two somehow related?

I looked out of the window at the moon in the red sky and pondered. There really was no way to tell whether it was Lucy who had taken the book out. The moon was massive tonight. I could tell when one day moved into another because of the moon. Throughout the day, it would get progressively bigger and bigger and closer and closer to the building. By midday, it would be so enormous that I could practically see the individual craters on it. Then it would retract further and further into the distance until the scarlet sky darkened into a deep burgundy colour. By midnight, it would be almost the size of a regular moon and the sky would be a red so deep as to be almost black. At that moment in the library, the moon was at its largest so I estimated it to be around midday. It looked like a massive eye staring accusingly at me through the smeared glass of the window. I stared it down for a while, an odd creeping feeling spreading throughout me, as if it could see me. My heart beat unsteadily inside my chest.

I spent the next few weeks poring over the book. It was fascinating. It wasn't like Lucy's spell books: cheap guides on how to light candles and put things in jars written by liberal-arts majors living in Massachusetts with seven dogs and a parakeet. It was almost scientific. It spoke of other worlds, dimensions invisible to the human mind. It likened the universe to a giant doll's house, and each plane of reality was a different room. Apparently there were countless rooms in this house, stretching beyond human imagination. But the dolls inside were unaware of the other rooms. The book also postulated that, if the mind was properly trained, then it was possible to move around a room, or even between rooms, using rituals and the power of the mind.

Soon I had read the entire hefty tome. It was a strange book. I kept coming across pages I thought I had read earlier and nothing ever seemed to be in the place it had previously been. Then I began to practise. I focused my mind and perfected the incantations, practising for most of the day. My head strained from having to remember everything: from the delicate movements of my hands to the rhythm of the words I had to utter. Sometimes, I would feel something rise up inside me like a volcano about to erupt. Every nerve in my body would tingle like static electricity. But then I'd make a minuscule error and the feeling would dissipate like dust in the wind.

One night, I was beginning to feel quite desperate, and knew I needed sleep. I remembered Lucy: her soft, slightly tangled hair falling over her eyes as she crouched on my bed and wriggled her toes on my bedspread. I remembered her talking about her trips to the psychiatrist. 'She told me the same old stuff,' she had said. 'About how I don't have to push myself to be perfect and that it's OK to go at my own pace.' She'd gazed down at her bare, dirty feet and extended them to trace patterns in my grubby carpet. 'It's annoying hearing the same things over and over again, but...' She'd sighed and smiled up at me with her deep blue eyes. 'I know she's not wrong. It's silly how I feel like I have to prove myself to everyone.' I hadn't known what to say so I simply held her hand. Her soft gaze met mine. 'It's OK to go at your own pace.'

'It's OK to go at your own pace,' I mumbled to myself, gazing down at my hand. I dragged my aching body to bed and fell into a deep sleep. I dreamt of words spoken in different languages, and of tumbling feathers and of moons that were really big blue eyes. When I awoke, it was the next evening. I felt inexplicably peaceful. I could see all the incantations and symbols so clearly in my own mind. I drew the circle on the floor and, closing my eyes, said the words. I sensed the something rise up inside me until it filled my whole body. I thought of the moon and how it looked like an eye. I imagined the moon blinking and becoming a clear blue eye. I spoke the words that felt like a roar emitting from deep inside me, experienced a brief feeling of complete weightlessness, and when I opened my eyes I was in the foyer of the library.

It is a peculiar thing to discover you can teleport using only the power of the mind. I was dumbfounded. Everyone imagines what they'd do if they had superpowers but I was so alarmed by my newfound ability that I didn't attempt to replicate it for another couple of days. Yet I couldn't get any of it out of my mind: the peaceful, clear-headed feeling; the something rising in my throat or the sensation of weightlessness. My whole body tingled with the thrill of it.

On the third day, I attempted it again. It took a couple of tries but, eventually, my body rang like a bell and I opened my eyes to find myself in the library foyer once more. I had performed the miracle twice. I felt my face slowly stretch into a grin that threatened to split my cheeks in half. I let out a loud whoop and did a spontaneous cartwheel before lying flat on my back and letting laughs of joy wrack my body.

Over the following months, I practised over and over again. It didn't work every time. Sometimes, it would be entire weeks before I could get it to work again. Once or twice, I tried it only to find myself losing the weightless feeling too soon, falling out of the air and landing with a jolt in some random area of the building, as if the ritual hadn't functioned properly. I had lost track of time by this point but I suspected I had been in the red-sky dimension for about a year and a half before I perfected the process. By that point, I could transport anywhere in the university campus with little effort.

I grew bold with my newly acquired powers. If I was able to transport anywhere in the same room in the doll's house, then why couldn't I find my way into another room? In the back of the *Occultus* was a long list of various dimensions that it was possible to travel to. The name of each dimension had a single sentence written next to it which presumably described the dimension. They were often quite oblique: 'The Realm of Silent Sleep', or 'The Dimension of the Two Beasts'. Sometimes they made no sense at all: 'Too Many Sheep Mouths' or 'Where the Tiger Drives the Snow'. I wondered which one could be the dimension I came from. I had long ago learned not to raise my hopes, but my heart couldn't help but pound while reading them, as the possibility that I could return home loomed large in my mind. Once I felt I had perfected my powers of transportation I pored over the list of dimensions, trying to decipher which could possibly be mine. I studied the book long into the night until I came across something that made my tired eyes snap open. There was a dimension listed named 'Lanicrom', and the description next to it read 'Blue and green'. That could only mean planet Earth! I really should have thought my reasoning through a little, but I was just so desperate to get home that I was willing to jump at the first possible option that presented itself. Hands shaking, I drew the circle and took my place in the centre of it. I spoke the words, moved my hands and felt the sensation of weightlessness.

In an instant, I knew something was wrong. I opened my eyes but all I could see was bright flashes of blue and green that stung my retinas. I grunted in pain and closed my eyes but the colours still scorched my eyelids like fireworks. It was like looking directly into the sun. There was no air in my lungs and my body felt sore and strained as if it was being mercilessly squeezed in a giant fist. I appeared to be floating, as if there was nothing solid in this dimension. Panicking, I felt for the chalk in my pocket. I didn't know if I would live long enough to do the incantation but I nonetheless tried tracing the outline of the transportation circle in the air in front of me. A particularly bright flash of green exploded behind my eyelids and I cried out in pain, or at least would have if there had been any air inside me. I realised with horror that I had dropped the chalk, and my body was too numb to reach out and search for it. After a few moments I felt strangely peaceful. This wasn't exactly how I had pictured myself dying, but at least after this there would be no more loneliness, no more red skies, no more crows... and no more Lucy. In the corner of my mind I saw an eye; a big blue eye, as wide and unblinking as the moon. I pictured the eye in the centre of the casting circle as I spoke the words without opening my mouth. The rush rose from deep inside me, I was weightless for an instant, and then I landed with a crash on the floor of the university basement. I lay there, aching and winded as the crackle of the ham radio buzzed in the air.

I was seriously shaken by this experience. I realised there was no way to tell which dimension listed in the *Occultus* was mine. I could keep trying, transporting to one at a time until, by process of elimination, I found my way home. But I could not tell whether I would once again end up somewhere like the blue-and-green dimension. It had become apparent that there were rooms in the doll's house that were completely unable to support human life. I had barely escaped with my life last time, and was in no hurry to try it again.

I settled back into my old routine of waking, eating, reading and stretching... I became acclimatised to it much more quickly this time. I didn't really feel despair any longer. I suppose I was resigned to the fact that I might never escape this place. One afternoon, I found myself in the cafeteria once more. The shadows had all disappeared and were probably in the classrooms. I had Joseph Pak's notebook in front of me and was doodling in the margins. The *Occultus* was lying a few feet away from me on the table. I stared at it for a moment before reaching out and pulling it towards me. I flipped slowly through the pages until I reached the list of dimensions at the back. I stared at them for what seemed like hours. Then I took the pen I had been using to draw in the notebook and scored out the first name and its matching description. That felt good. I did it again, scoring out the second name so hard it tore through the paper. I went through the book methodically, scoring out each dimension as I went. My movements became more and more frenzied as I flipped the pages furiously, tearing them, and scribbling over entire sheets. Soon I was simply gouging pages with my pen as silent tears streamed down my face. This book had been my last hope of getting home and I didn't even know how to use it. Dull desperation lay like a lead weight in my heart as I stabbed at the *Occultus*'s fraying pages. Suddenly, I stopped. Something had caught my eye. In the centre of one of the pages was the name of a dimension, listed as 'Marinus' with a description that read 'The Realm of Hearts.' That wasn't remarkable in itself. But next to the entry, drawn in felt-tip and lovingly shaded in with coloured pencils, was a little red heart with a pair of wings sprouting from its sides and a gold crown perched on top of it. Precisely the same heart that Lucy used to draw at the bottom of all her notes.

I gazed at it with teary eyes. A strange feeling gestated in my gut at the sight of Lucy's symbol. I took the pen and scratched another transformation circle in the floor. I had somehow been able to teleport without one when

I escaped the Lanicrom dimension but I was too shaken to attempt it again, so I resolved to rely on the tried-and-tested method for the time being. I sat cross-legged in the middle of the chalk circle and spoke the words. I could sense the moon outside the window staring down at me. I imagined a blue eye once again, along with blonde hair, freckles, a soft voice and countless other things. And a heart with wings flying through the air. My body felt as though it was flooded with light as I became weightless once more.

I opened my eyes and had to shut them again. I was dizzy and disorientated. The journey must have been a strain on me. I took some deep breaths and opened my eyes. I wasn't dizzy any longer but felt strangely light-headed. I had been in my dimensional prison for so long that I hadn't realised how heavy and oppressive the air was there. It had been like wading through a hot, wet jungle and had made me drowsy and unfocused. The air in this new dimension was so soft, so clear and so fresh and light that the first intake of breath had made me feel faintly disjointed. It was like emerging from a sauna.

Once I had found my bearings, I realised that I was in what appeared to be Lecture Hall 3, where the science seminars were held. I looked up at the clock. To my utter delight, it appeared to be working. I watched the hands move steadily for five minutes. The clock now read 8:25 p.m. I wondered why I felt so uneasy. Then I realised just how quiet it was. So deathly quiet that the air hummed with silence. It was a welcome relief from the crows but it unnerved me all the same. I looked down in front of me. The book had travelled with me and lay on the stained carpet, pages open at the spell that had transported me here. I closed the book and hid it under the lecturer's desk. I then walked out of the lecture hall and into the corridor, my footsteps echoing like thunderclaps.

That's when I saw it.

The sky. It was black. Not just a starless night, but moonless as well. Devoid of any colour, even the faint shades that can usually be found threaded throughout darkness. It was sheer darkness. The absence of light, of colour, of anything. The university grounds lay before me, void of crows, but they were slowly breaking up, crumbling into gravel and disappearing into the void. There was a low rumbling in the air. I stared out of the window for a while, wondering where I was. Had I made it back to my home dimension or had I ended up somewhere else? Suddenly, my stomach grumbled and in an instant I realised just how hungry I was. I wandered down to the cafeteria, passing all the same doors and corridors I used to pass in many months of confinement. There was no one to be seen anywhere. There weren't even any shadows. I was surprised to find myself actually missing them.

I entered the cafeteria and went to get a sandwich from the cold shelves, but when I reached them I saw that the power was off and all the food in the refrigerator had congealed. The only things that hadn't rotted away were the crisps which had stayed fresh in their protective foil wrapping. I picked up a packet of cheese and onion and sat down at a table to eat it. I finished the packet and considered what to do next. I thought about the book back in the lecture hall.

I was just considering trying another dimension when I heard a clanking sound coming from a nearby broom cupboard. I froze, my body singing in horror. I picked up a chair and slowly advanced on the cupboard. Shaking, I threw open the door, saw what was inside and dropped the chair on to the floor. I stood there, trembling and staring at the figure lying on the floor in front of me clutching a mop like a sword.

It was Lucy. Her hair was matted and her dress hung loosely off her slight frame. Her face was set in a threatening grimace, her teeth bared. When she saw me, her mouth fell open and her mop fell with a clatter to the ground. My eyes pricked with tears as she ran into my arms and clasped me to her. I stiffened for a moment, unsure whether I was dreaming or not. But no: Lucy was really in my arms. It was Lucy's hair, Lucy's scent, Lucy's warmth… I let my body succumb to exhaustion and wrapped my aching, tired body around hers as we both fell into a heap on the floor.

I sat cross-legged on a table across from Lucy, sharing a bottle of wine she'd found in a lecturer's office. 'I was trying to make it last until the end,' she said, taking a long swig. 'But I think this is a reason to celebrate.' She gave me a lopsided grin that made my heart turn over. I wanted to pull her into my arms again but I needed answers.

'What do you mean, "the end"?' My voice was raspy from not talking for so long. She lowered her voice to match mine. Our tiny voices echoed throughout the silent building.

'You see, I was in kind of a bad way from my parents' divorce. It felt like... I didn't belong anywhere all of a sudden.' She looked embarrassed. 'I know this all sounds incredibly frivolous now, but at the time I was pretty torn up about it.' I reached out and squeezed her hands. She gave me a wan smile and continued. 'I was hanging out in the library when I saw this awesome-looking book being returned by that cute, neurotic Korean guy. You know, the one from your history class?'

I nodded 'Joseph Pak.' I scowled. 'You really think he's cute?'

Lucy grinned mischievously at me. 'Anyway, the "cute-but-not-as-cute-as-you" Joseph Pak returned this big, dusty-looking book. It looked like something out of Dungeons and Dragons, and you know what a fantasy geek I am. So I just *had* to take it out.' Her eyes misted over as she remembered. 'That book became my life. I read it so many times. I learned how to teleport from place to place, and how to move through solid objects, stuff like that. I never dreamed that magic could actually exist. I... I started to get a bit drunk on it.' She paused, a look of shame coming over her face, and she took several more swigs of wine before continuing. 'I discovered this spell. It could only be used once but it could transport you to any point in time. I thought about the night Dad left, and how the last thing I said to him was how much I hated him and what a useless man he was.' Another pause, this time tearful. 'I wanted to travel back to that moment and say something a little more balanced. But...' She faltered.

'Luce, please tell me.' She shook her head.

'You'll never forgive me, Mark,' she said in a minuscule voice.

I laughed. 'Don't be silly. I'm just so, so happy to see you. So happy you're here. I'll forgive anything right now, I'm so happy.'

'Well, you see... I think... the spell may have backfired, just a tiny bit. I may have... ended the world. A little bit. A lot.' She lowered her head so I couldn't see her expression through her tangled hair. I looked out of the window at the slowly encroaching darkness.

'Well, that would explain a lot,' I said.

Lucy burst out laughing. The sound of her laughter was so beautiful that I couldn't stop myself from laughing too. We both laughed until our bodies were empty of any sound. We laughed hysterically, unable to stop. Somehow, we ended up in a giggling heap on the floor, limbs tangling with trembling limbs. We lay in each other's arms for a while. I stroked her hair as she rested her hands against my chest to hear my heartbeat. After a long silence, I said, 'So this is really home.'

'What's left of it,' Lucy mumbled and held me a little bit tighter. I traced circles in her frail back.

'Where *was* I, Luce?'

Lucy was silent for a minute or two. I felt her heart beating under her smooth ribcage. Then she spoke. 'Like I said, the time-travel spell could only be used once. I couldn't change my mistake. I wanted to save the people I cared about.' She shook a little in my arms but then took a deep breath and continued. 'I read about the Nexal dimension. In the book, it was listed as "The Realm of Lost Things". That sounded about right. I know I didn't really think things through, but I was scared.'

There were thousands of things I wanted to say to her but none of them wanted to come out of my mouth, so I simply kissed her shoulder and told her to continue. 'I used another spell to send you there first. But the *Occultus* disappeared with you, so I couldn't send the rest of my family. I'm sorry.'

Lucy began to cry the tears of a woman who has nothing left. We clung to each other as the world ended and my mind wandered. Something was bothering me.

'Luce? How long has the world been ending?'

'I'm not quite sure. I'd say about two months,' she said, trying to choke back her tears. 'Everybody ran to the hospitals and army bases when the stars started to break apart. I didn't want to face anyone so I holed myself up in here. As far as I can tell, I'm the only person left alive in this dimension, and the darkness looks like it's almost here.'

'But I've been in that place for at least two years. How has it only been a couple of months here?'

'I guess time moves faster in the Nexal than here,' Lucy muttered. She sounded exhausted.

'Go to sleep, baby,' I whispered into her hair. 'I'll be here when you wake up.'

'Don't be so sure,' Lucy said with a grin, indicating the crumbling world outside. She giggled shrilly and then fell asleep in an instant. I held her slumbering body as I imagined how things must have been for her over the past few months. I imagined her walking the hallways in despair as I had. I cried a little for her then. And for me. We'd both been through so much pain. Neither of us had a future. But at least we were together. I felt myself drifting off as the apocalypse rumbled closer and closer outside the window. I took a small glimmer of pleasure in the thought that the infernal book would be destroyed along with us.

The book!

My eyes snapped open and I shivered in excitement. 'Lucy. Lucy, wake up,' I said breathlessly as I shook her. She groaned in annoyance but opened her eyes. 'Haven't you wondered how I got back here?' She blinked up at me, bleary-eyed.

'So I suppose I'm not going to get to sleep through the end of the world after all,' she grumbled.

'It might not be the end.'

Lucy gazed out of the window at the black sky and then looked back at me, raising an eyebrow.

'OK, it might be the end of this universe, but it doesn't have to be the end of us.'

She stared up at me and I noticed a faint spark of hope flash in her deep blue eyes. I picked her up as gently as I could and pulled her by her hand up several flights of stairs to Lecture Hall 3. I let go of her hand and walked over to the desk. I presented the *Occultus* with a flourish.

Lucy's hands flew up to her mouth and her eyes grew wide as hubcaps. 'But... that's the... How did you get it?'

I shrugged. 'It must have come through to the Nexal with me.'

Lucy threw herself into me with her full force, almost knocking me over. She laughed with relief, tears welling up in her miraculously blue eyes. Then she went limp.

'But what can it *do*? I told you: the time-travel spell can only be used once. We can't go back and stop this from happening.' Her arms fell lamely by her side. 'Trust me, I've tried everything to stop this from happening.'

I reached out and lifted her chin. Her tearful gaze met mine. 'Maybe we could travel to another dimension,' I suggested.

Lucy blinked at me. 'Which one?'

'Any of them. We're bound to come across one similar to our own eventually. We'll just keep travelling until we come across one to settle down in.'

Lucy looked uncertain. I felt the same way, but I didn't want to show it in front of her. She needed me to be strong. At that precise moment, the entire building shook. We clung to each other until it passed. We looked at one another and realised that we didn't really have any alternative.

'Alright then,' said Lucy, turning the book to the appropriate page. She was shaking. I took her hand in mine.

'This could actually be brilliant, Luce. Think about it: a pair of magical lovers bound by destiny travelling across the stars hand-in-hand to find a new home.'

Lucy smiled at this. 'You old romantic.' She set about drawing a circle on the floor with a spare piece of chalk she had in her pocket. We sat across from each other and began to speak the words. The low hum of the end of the universe was slowly becoming a dull roar as it approached us.

She suddenly grabbed my hand and held it tight. 'Mark,' she said, her voice quivering. 'I'm scared.'

I took both her hands in mine and gazed into her eyes. 'Me too, Lucy. But I like being scared.' I shot her what I hoped was a rakish grin. 'As long as it's with you.' I waggled my eyebrows.

She pretended to scoff at me, her cheeks turning pink. 'You always were a bit of an idiot.' Then she smiled tenderly. 'But you're *my* idiot.'

I leaned forward and kissed her. It was the last kiss that would ever take place in this dimension. And it wasn't at all a bad one to go out on, all things considered.

We sat across from each other and closed our eyes, speaking the words as the universe let out a last dying roar. As I felt our bodies begin to fill with light, I prayed that, wherever we ended up, there would always be Lucy and her deep blue eyes.

And that there would be no crows.

THE LAST TREE

SARAH

Another tour guide, on the hour, pulls up beside me.

'This is the Living Natural History Exhibit. All these species are now the last of their kind. We rescued them from the wild. Nature is now extinct outside this museum. Natural species were unable to adapt to the needs of society.'

'We rescued them!'

You destroyed us. If you hadn't destroyed us, you wouldn't have had to rescue us. 'It's all your bloody fault,' I shout back at them. That's it. I've had enough. If they aren't going to tell the truth, I'm damn well going to try. As the next tour draws up next to me I take a deep breath and gather my thoughts.

'Hello, and welcome to the Natural History Museum. I am the big and mighty Gregor – the last tree on Earth. You may be asking yourselves right now, how am I the last tree on Earth, when trees used to cover 30 per cent of the world's surface?' I pause and wait for the nods. The humans aren't responding the way I wanted. I should continue, that's what the tour guides normally do when it seems none of the humans are listening to them. 'Well, what a brilliant question. The answer is: YOU!

You destroyed the whole natural world. Our homes, our families. You killed my best friend Mags. Look around this glass dome. The plants here are the last of their kind. You're here to admire them, to look at their colours and say how beautiful they are, to enjoy yourself for a day. Then you go home at night and forget about us, while we stay here. We are your prisoners.'

They're not listening. Let's talk about something that they *will* like, like how clever they've been in their quest to destroy nature.

'The dome – well, I don't know what it's made of, but what I do know is that there is no way I can escape from it. I've tried a thousand times. I grow bigger and bigger and sometimes the humans don't notice or don't care. I push my branches against the dome and I get pushed back. Another trick I've tried is to build up some momentum. Every so often the humans have air pumped into the dome, mainly in the summer. Sometimes my smaller branches pick up the wind that blows through, and occasionally I hit the dome, but never hard enough. The dome is very strong. Too strong. Congratulations! Your prisoners will not escape.

'You control everything. After many years in your company I am fully aware of your need to have control. Well, in here, you have the ultimate control. Everything from the water I drink, to the food I eat, to the view I have is given to me by humans. Oh, and you have a specific time to give me each of these necessary life-giving tools throughout the day. According to you, I am thirsty three times a day – once when the lights go on, once during the day and then as soon as the lights go out. That's all rubbish! The lights you humans installed shine so brightly and hum when they're on. When my leaves get too close to the ever-white beaming lights they get scorched and fall off. So that's your dome.

'Now I bet you're thinking, what use is a tree? Trees were essential to human life, before you were self-sufficient from nature. Us trees used to keep the air supply clean and full of oxygen. Yes, that's right, we were *your* provider. And did you know that I could produce around 117 kilograms of oxygen per year? That's loads, by the way. That's enough to keep two humans alive for a year. And that's just me. But now you've created a system where you produce your own oxygen and you don't need trees. We had other jobs too, but you never appreciated them. Wait, wait – come back! Don't go away.'

The group is leaving. They either didn't like my speech or they can't hear me. Next time I'll just have to speak louder.

I recycle the speech as the humans do in their tours until the last ones leave. Finally, the lights that burn me go out, and I am alone. I look around and convince myself that this will be the last day I'm held captive. I tell myself that tomorrow they'll decide to set me free, into the world I used to live in. I look around the dome. All I see is the reflection of what I have become. The last tree.

I stretch to reach the top of this white reflective cage. My dull freckled leaves brush against the cool surface of the glass that holds me in. I stand at twenty-five feet, if you count my leaves and the small twigs, which I do – and proudly protrude in every direction. I look at my cage and think about how lovely it will be when they come to set me free. When I can feel the warmth radiating from the life-giving source of the sun against the surface of my moss-encrusted branches. My leaves will find relief in changing to their vibrant colours. In this cage, the weather never changes – the heating constantly on, my leaves devoid of any sort of meaningful life. It makes me long for the change of season. The naked freeze of winter to the fresh days of spring bringing blossoming buds and baby birds, and then into the vitality of summer, when my branches can't be seen thanks to the lush greenery that covers me. Then to autumn, my favourite season, when my leaves turn to fire, blazing reds and yellows, only to fall with every breath of wind. And once more to winter when I'm left a silhouette.

The dome makes me feel so alone. Communicating with the other plants is difficult. Not only did the humans capture me, but my roots are contained in some unbreakable material. No roots connected to anything means no talking. Did the humans intend this or don't they understand me? Either way, the situation doesn't change. I've gradually become used to my own company. The days aren't so bad. The nights are the worst.

The darkness brings my dreams, or more often my nightmares. The best dream is of when I was free, when all was calm in our tree community. The nightmares bring back the day I was pulled down – the moment I saw the humans destroy my Mags.

Mags was my soulmate. We grew up together as saplings surrounded by a community of trees. She was the most beautiful of them all, with her silver bark sparkling in the moonlight. She was unusually delicate in her appearance. Her branches weren't like mine, rigid and bulky. Mags' branches had bright green leaves. They hung and gently flowed with the lightest breeze, as though she was dancing.

Our peaceful community was destroyed when the humans started to build their nests in our forest. At first, they chose to put their nests on the bare land outside, but over time they came closer and eventually I ended up here. The first day the humans invaded, they took down ten trees. I saw them tying what looked like long ropes around one of the oldest. He had stood in our community since the beginning. The ropes went all the way to his crown. A human then started using the ropes to climb up him, a machine dangling from his hips. When the human got to the outside branches of my dear friend, he switched on the machine. It choked violently and the cutting silver teeth started to spin faster and faster, tearing away at him. This was a human activity we were used to. The humans had to make us look a certain way and help us grow in a way that was appropriate for them – more proof that humans love control.

The human moved so fast. Within two swipes of the silver blade a branch fell to the ground, and then another and another, until the old tree was left with his trunk bare, carnage all around him. I knew this wasn't normal and I started to panic. A larger machine was brought out to cut through the trunk quickly, with some humans on the ground pulling on the top rope. My friend smashed to the forest floor. All that was left was a stump. I tried to peer over at what was happening as the humans crowded around. It looked like they were putting four holes in my friend's stump and filling them up with some kind of liquid. Almost immediately I could hear screams from the trees around him. 'He's dead. His roots are dead. They're killing us.'

Everything fell silent, until the humans broke it with their next kill. The birds and the other mammals we lived with never did this. They didn't destroy us to build their homes – they lived with us. Why couldn't the humans do that as well?

As each tree stump was dug up its bare roots were shamelessly exposed to the world. Soon the land in front of me was barren. I had lost most of my friends but the humans kept going. I realised then it would only be a matter of time before they got to me and Mags. The shock of seeing the brutal attacks on my friends made me shiver, and the pigment in my leaves faded. When the first trees were cut, sap oozed from my trunk and I couldn't speak for days. Eventually there was no sap left. All I could think was that Mags and I were next.

I stayed awake most nights hoping that I would never hear the crunching and roaring of the cutting machine.

I kept a careful lookout for human activity and warned the others when I saw the humans come back again. I became obsessed with Mags. I wanted to protect her. I became convinced that if I was going to die, I wanted my last image to be of her. I could see the humans' nests getting closer. Their tree-destroying machines moved nearer each day and haunted us at night. I knew that tomorrow would once again be a killing day.

And it was: I woke to the sound of the rattling and raving machines. The humans move at a faster speed than us trees – a second to a tree can be minutes for a human. I could tell the machine was close to me, and they were sawing into one of us, but so far I felt no pain. The worst thing about being a tree is that you don't feel pain until minutes or sometimes even hours after a cut. I waited for the pain to start and hoped it wouldn't last long.

I saw the quick motion of a blade swipe across the nearest of Mags' branches. It fell to the ground and I screamed.

'Mags. Mags! Can you hear me? Are you okay? Mags?' I waited to hear something – anything – but nothing came. I searched for our connecting roots. Why couldn't I hear her? Why wasn't she there? Suddenly I felt her root pull away from mine. 'No. Mags, don't do this.' My roots continued to search for hers as the humans destroyed her. I knew I only had a few more moments to connect with her.

I will forever be haunted by the image of Mags' beautiful branches collapsing onto one another, forming a pile on the floor. Her leaves falling, and the abandoned nest that had held last year's birds scattered amongst the wreckage.

I had never wanted to be a human, but on that day, that's exactly what I wanted. Humans were cold-blooded and heartless, and felt no guilt about being so. They knew nothing of the distress they were causing. Maybe if they looked up they would see my furious shaking and it would make them stop, but it probably only looked like the wind blowing my branches from side to side. As I shook I felt my leaves fall to join Mags' on the floor. Tears of sap ran down through my trunk as I realised I was losing her.

After being beside me for hundreds of years, Mags was no longer there. I finally caught one of her roots and held it tight. She was screaming as her roots scrambled through the soil. I held onto them as the humans poured the killing liquid into the four holes in her stump.

'It's going to be okay, Mags. It's… going to be quick. I'll be here the whole time. I'll never let go of you.' I felt her roots become cold and start to shrink. She was quiet and still. I held on as tight as I could. 'Mags. I'm sorry. I love you!' I screamed, as she was yanked away from my grasp and dragged from the ground.

I watched the wind sweep away her leaves for the rest of the day. I hoped that tomorrow the humans would cut me down so I could join her.

The machines started up in the morning and I didn't care. Gradually all my leaves and branches joined Mags' on the ground. I didn't feel any pain at first, but gradually it caught up with me. Soon it was overwhelming, but I just screamed at them.

'Come on, humans! Do your worst!' My voice faltered as the humans cut my trunk at the top. This was going to be it. 'You believe you're winning, but you're not. You need me, you need all of us more than you know. And one day it will be your families. Remember this. You're killing your future.' I fell silent as I remembered that it didn't matter about the humans. What mattered was that I was going to be with Mags. I saw the next part of my knobbly trunk fall. Suddenly the humans stopped. I was a stump, but hadn't yet been cut short enough to kill me.

'Wait. What's happening? You're meant to kill me, so I can be with Mags. KILL ME! I want to die, I want you to kill me right now.' The new machine had thicker ropes which they tied to me, tighter than the ropes they'd climbed up. Then they started to dig around my roots, being careful not to hurt me. The ropes started to pull me up from the ground. Was I being moved? 'No, you can't do this. YOU CAN'T DO THIS TO ME!' Sap leaked from every inch of me as my roots were exposed to the air, sending chills through me.

They dragged me and only me to this glass prison.

Today brought with it the usual boring things. Lights on, sprinklers on (I wasn't thirsty but the humans have their routine) and the tours started. People's blank faces always look the same, two round dots just staring at me, a few nods here and there as they hear the speech. One girl in the first group today asks, 'Why was nature on the earth in the first place?'

The leader of the group turns and smiles. 'There was a time when we needed nature. Not anymore.'

'You still need us,' I tell her, 'otherwise you wouldn't have a job.' This group disappears into the next room and the next mob comes along. I watch as the humans look at me, scanning me up and down. I do the same to them.

In this next group a boy stands at the front staring at me. He smiles at me, directly at me. He's taken out a small black stick which moves fast on a white square leaf. I see his eyes moving quickly between me and his leaf, scanning every inch of me for something. I do the same to him. His eyes are like the sky and he moves like Mags, like he's dancing. I've never experienced anyone watching me so intensely. The group moves on as usual after the chatty tour lady finishes, but the boy stays, his eyes fixed on me.

Eventually he stops and looks at his leaf, raises it up in front of him, and then turns it around for me to see. It's a perfect black and white version of me.

'Don't you think it looks like you, mate?' the boy whispers. His blue eyes open wide as he nods his head towards the black-and-white version of me. Is he talking to me? Does he know that I can see him, that I can hear him? I want to speak to him but a severe-looking woman approaches him. 'Come on, keep up. The assignment is about the whole exhibit, not just the tree. Which means you need to listen to what the tour guide is telling you.' She smiles. 'You'll have time to do your own research before we head back to school.' The boy just nods. I want him to leave the black-and-white version of me but he shoves it in his bag and wipes his hands on his red-and-blue stripy T-shirt, which leaves a black smear. He turns to me and winks. He knows I'm here. 'Tomorrow,' he mouths at me. 'I'm going to try and come back tomorrow.'

I try to recall whether I know him from somewhere. He's too young to have known me when I was in the wild. I've been here for about fifty years. Could he have come on the tour before? I spend the rest of the day looking out for him, but he doesn't come back. The day continues with the same boring groups of humans and tour guides.

The lights go out as usual when all the humans leave. It's dark in here but I can see around the whole circular cage because some moonlight shines through. As I grew bigger in my prison I found that my image was reflected in the glass around me in every direction, a 360° version of me. Even though in reality I'm the only tree, it looks like there are hundreds of trees in here. A forest of me. I pretend I'm with my friends and Mags in our community. Sometimes I smile at the images on the glass walls and they smile back. Then we wave to each other from across the room. For a moment, I forget where I am. Perhaps that's silly, but it helps me get through the nights. Tonight is different though – for the first time since being here I'm excited about waking up tomorrow. I don't mind going to sleep. I'm not thinking about being the last tree and how I would rather be dead. I just want to see the boy again; I want to speak to him. Maybe he can give the humans a message for me.

It feels like a moment has passed, but I've been dreaming for hours. I've been woken up by feet stamping quickly up my trunk. It's a human.

'Get off me – get OFF me!'

Why are they doing this? Are they going to cut me down again?

'I must see the boy again, because he saw me. He knows about me, he knows I'm here. You can't do this to me.'

The human has stopped and sat down where my trunk splits into its three main branches. I breathe in deeply. This isn't normal for the cage. In the wild humans sometimes climbed me, but that was when we were outside. I wait to see what the human does next. He breathes. I breathe. He slumps down into my trunk. I relax slightly as well. He throws his jacket to the floor. I throw a leaf. The human seems familiar but in this dim light it's hard to really know. All humans look so similar.

'Told you I would be back.'

It's him. The boy. He's here.

'I wonder what it's like to be the last of your kind,' he says. 'If I were the last human alive, I'd find a way of setting you free, that's for sure. And all the other creatures. You know it's not just you, kept prisoner like this. Everything that was called nature has ended up like you. It should be against the law or something – that's what I think. But no one listens to me.'

'You know what, they don't listen to me either if that helps,' I reply. 'I tell them I'm full of water and they pour loads more on. I feel like I'm drowning half the time. And you know the lights in here? They're horrible. I can't believe they've done this to nature. I remember the days when everything was wild. And my ancestors told me stories of when the humans ruled nothing, when nature ruled them – when they feared nature.' The boy looks amazed, and I smile. 'Can you hear me?'

'I wonder whether you saw the first human on Earth?'

'Look, I know I look old, but seriously – that's taking the micky a bit. I'm a couple of hundred years old.'

The boy suddenly jumps down from me and walks over to the sign that stands next to me. He shines a light on it.

'I saw this earlier but I wasn't paying attention to that tour lady. They're so patronising here, saying how they saved you. Though actually they probably did, after what we did to the environment. It says here you're two hundred and fifty years old. Wow. That's old. You must have been the oldest tree ever. That would be so amazing. Is that why they chose you?' The boy climbs back up to his perch, laughing.

'No, hold on a minute. That's not old! I knew of a tree called Methuselah who was nearly five thousand years old. I've heard of trees nearly ten thousand years old as well. So I'm like you. I'm YOUNG! And chosen.

I'm not sure why I was chosen or put in here. But most days I wish they'd killed me.' I sink slightly as I realise I'd already told him my age but he still had to look at the sign, meaning he couldn't hear me after all. Maybe I'm just meant to listen.

'I bet you're really interesting to talk to. I bet you would have loads of stories to tell me. You'd be more interesting than all the books put together.'

It's been so long since I could tell someone a story. I used to tell Mags stories all the time to help her go to sleep, especially once the humans started purging the community. I particularly like romantic stories, the ones where everyone is happy and in love, just like me and Mags.

'A story. I can tell you a story.' The boy doesn't object. 'I could tell you how I met Mags. My Mags was the most beautiful of all the trees I had ever seen. She was placed next to me as a sapling. She grew into the most wonderful friend and she was amazing to look at, especially in the sunset, because the sun gently sparkled off her silver bark and onto the grass beneath her. Anyway, we'd been friends for a long time but I had never told her how I felt, until this one night. Some humans came along. They spent hours decorating the gap between me and Mags. At the end of the day there was an arch that joined me and Mags together. They had used other materials to do it but my branch was helping to keep it up, and so was Mags' We were touching for the first time. It took my breath away and we both smiled at each other. A group of people wearing the most beautiful colourful clothing stood around marvelling at us, and two men stood just beneath our arch. A woman wearing a long white dress, her hair flowing freely behind her with only some flowers to keep it off her face, came and stood under the arch. The three humans stood between us with other humans watching as they proclaimed their love for each other. Someone read out statements that said whatever happened they promised to stay with each other forever, and after each statement the couple said, "I do." They smiled the whole way through and at the end they exchanged rings and kissed each other. I could see that Mags was leaking sap everywhere as she danced her flowing branches around in celebration for the humans' union. That's when I told her that one day she and I would be united together forever.'

As I finish talking the boy turns to the branch to his right and hugs me. 'It must have been a beautiful story.' This boy is so young. It's unusual; normally boys his age don't care about me. Forget that – he's unusual for any human. Their whole species doesn't seem to care, whatever age they are. Maybe I have a friend again.

'Boy, what's happened tonight?' The boy doesn't answer and I realise how stupid I was to even ask in the first place. Then he starts to cry.

'It's alright, I'm here. I know you probably can't hear me but you can talk to me, you know.' After a few moments, all my hopes of reaching him fade. I just look at him and make one of my big leaves fall on top of him. I see him pick it up and rub his nose with it, and his eyes. I like that. He holds onto the leaf as if it's a gift.

'I feel trapped. I feel that I'm alone and no one in this world gets me or understands me.' Is he reading my mind? Is it possible that a human is feeling and experiencing everything that I'm going through, I wonder? 'I keep trying to understand this stupid place but I don't. People keep telling me that I'm wrong and I keep trying to do things differently to make up for the fact that I'm just wrong. Nothing seems to work. I don't have any friends; everyone thinks I'm a loser. I hate this place.' His voice is cracking. I can feel the water from his eyes fall onto my bark and I try to absorb it as quickly as it pours out of him. I wonder if this is helping him.

'You know my mum works here, she's in charge – you've probably met her. She's the really uptight bossy one who thinks everything that anyone does is no good and she knows best.' I can't help but let out a laugh. My leaves loosen up at this thought as he basically describes most humans I've ever met – it hasn't exactly narrowed down the choice of potential mums. 'She thinks that everything I do is wrong. I go to school and do my homework and for some reason that isn't good enough, because I haven't got a good enough grade. I show her my artwork and say to her that all I want to do is draw. She tells me I'm stupid to think that I could ever be an artist, that I don't have the talent, hard work and discipline to do such a thing. But she doesn't know me. She doesn't see the hours of hard work I put in developing my skills, the hours of pleasure that taking that piece of charcoal to a sheet of paper gives me. She doesn't see how much I could do with this skill. Instead she threw away all my art books and art equipment and told me enough was enough, I had to stop it. She told me I had to start being someone she could be proud of, stop being strange around others, stop absorbing myself in drawings and paintings, stop being myself and start being like everyone else. START BEING NORMAL. I just want to be who I naturally am but my mum won't let me.'

Yes, exactly. I too just want to be who I naturally am. But she won't let me either.

The boy is crying his heart out to me and all I want to do is put my branches around him and tell him that everything is going to be okay, that I understand. But I'm no use in this situation. He can't hear me, and I can't move for him. All I can do is stand here and listen. He sinks into my trunk and lays his head onto one of my branches. I feel him start to breathe slower and his tears stop falling on me. I think he's asleep.

I hope I've helped in some way, even if it was just by being here.

THE CLOCKMAKER

ESTHER LOWERY

The pocket-watch looks nearly completely broken.

Carefully, I remove the back and examine the gears inside. One's completely shattered and I gently pull out the bits and toss them away. The rest aren't in particularly good condition either. A few cracks, very rusty, although possibly still usable, if I can replace that one gear.

I drop my head against the wagon of cabbages I've been hiding behind for the past few hours. The air above is thick and smoggy. It's a little easier to breathe closer to the ground. Through the smog, I can just about see the grey clouds hanging overhead. I look back to the pocket-watch. I can't fix it, not here anyway. I don't have the tools or the gears necessary. Maybe I can ask Mr McCail.

I turn the pocket-watch around and run my fingers over the cracked front. I scavenged it from some rich chap's rubbish. He threw it away, deeming it to be of no more use. The face is painted in shiny black ink with delicate blue forget-me-nots painted around the numbers. Even broken, it's beautiful; it must've been splendid when it worked.

Sighing, I put it in my pocket and return to the bag of watches Mr McCail gave me to clean. I take one out, a rusty watch that might have been made of silver. The surface is rough where I run my fingers over the back, but I can feel indentations from now-faded writing.

I pull out my cloth and start to scrub at it, before I stop and look up.

Clip-clop-clip-clop.

The sound of hooves tapping against the cobbles comes down the street, followed by the rattle of carriage wheels.

It's not usual to hear that around here.

I turn, frowning at the black carriage bouncing along. The cabbie doesn't look lost. He's eagle-eyed and alert, fully aware of where he's going.

I put the pocket-watch down, my fingers curling around the wagon as I carefully stand up and watch the carriage move past me. Inside, I catch a glimpse of two people, a woman in a blue silk dress with silver hair bound under a big blue hat and a man with equally silver hair and the smartest black suit I've ever seen.

The woman is gazing outside, her eyes glassy and empty. They meet mine and for a split second we stare at each other before the carriage moves on.

A dirty boy runs up to the window. He has no shoes, no hat and his face is almost invisible under the soot.

'Spare a ha'penny for a poor young lad, eh?' he says, holding out his hands to the window, stumbling in his attempts to keep up.

A disgusted grunt comes from inside the carriage. A white, silk-gloved hand comes out of the window to shove the boy backwards. He falls, slamming into the cobbled street.

The boy doesn't cry. He's had worse no doubt, but he does glare up at the carriage as it moves on.

If they're not here to be *charitable*, which is another word for making themselves feel good without actually doing anything, then what are a pair of toffs doing here?

The carriage continues down the street. The boy scowls and shoves himself to his feet. 'Cor!' he yells. 'You're a bunch of rotters, aren't you?' He glares after it for a moment, before grabbing a stone and throwing it at the carriage with all his might. It misses, flying past the carriage and hitting the horse's rump.

The horse rears. The cabbie cries out, trying to get the horse under control, but as he does so the carriage rocks violently. Something falls out of the window, slamming into the mud underneath.

Apparently, no one notices, as the horse is controlled and the carriage continues on. The boy sends another dark look after it, before turning and running off. Once he's gone and the carriage turns the corner, I snatch up my bag of watches and run to look at what fell out, dropping into a kneel, ignoring where my skirts brush the mud.

It's a package of letters, crumpled and dirty, but still clearly legible. I stare after the carriage, before shoving the letters under my waistcoat, standing up and running as quickly as I can in the opposite direction, catching my skirts in my hands as I go.

I duck down alleyways, slipping past beggars and men in long coats until I finally reach my destination. It's a small, crooked building, listing to the left slightly like it's a bit tipsy. The windows are clouded and dirty and the sign hanging just above the door reads MR MCCAIL's CLOCKMAKERS.

I pause for a second, staring up at the sign. I can still remember first coming here, after my mother died, hoping for a small job. Mr McCail has given me so much more. A job, yes, though far bigger than I had expected; something just shy of a full apprenticeship. But, more than anything else, he's given me clocks. And that's more than I can ever repay.

I push the door open, the wind-chime ringing as the draught hits it. 'Mr McCail?' I call, stepping inside. The letters under my waistcoat burn like a hot poker.

The interior of the clockmaker's is about as grubby as the outside, but still homely somehow. Clocks of all shapes and sizes hang from the walls, all ticking away. The sound is soothing and smooth, a little like coming home.

A counter separates the rest of the shop from the place where customers come. I wander forward and knock on the counter. 'Mr McCail, you here?'

'Ah, Miss Prescott.' Mr McCail finally comes out of the back and leans on the counter, grinning widely. He's a fairly old man, with a very bald head and a twisted moustache over a normally smiling mouth. 'You've returned. Finished with those watches I gave you to clean?'

I nod, holding out the bag and steadfastly refusing to think about the letters under my waistcoat.

'Yes, sir,' I say. 'Some of them were a bit stubborn, but I got them all.'

Mr McCail smiles and takes the bag, looking over the watches inside. They're as clean as I can make them, although not necessarily working. But that's his job, not mine. 'Very good,' he says, once he finishes looking. He rummages about under the counter for a minute, before pulling out a money bag. 'We agreed two shillings, yes?'

I nod, leaning forward on my toes as he reaches into the bag.

'Aye.'

Mr McCail pulls out the coins and drops them into my hand, pulling himself up to sit on his countertop as I pocket the shillings. 'There you go,' he says, putting the bag back under the counter. 'You did good work here. I don't have anything at the moment, but if you need any more work, I'll happily get you to clean any more watches I might have in the future.'

I nod eagerly. 'Yes, sir!' Any money is a good thing and there are very few things I like more than playing with clockwork.

Mr McCail smiles. 'Come back in a few weeks,' he says. 'I might have some more then.'

It's a clear dismissal if ever I heard one, but I don't leave. I just shift in place, reaching for my pocket.

Mr McCail raises an eyebrow at me. 'What is it?' he asks.

I pull out the broken pocket watch. 'I found this in some fellow's rubbish and I wanted to know if you could fix it,' I say, all in a rush, the words tumbling out and over each other so that it's a wonder they all come out in the right order.

He raises an eyebrow and reaches out. I hand him the watch, ignoring the part of me that doesn't want anyone but me to touch it. He raises it and looks carefully at it, pulling out a magnifying glass in order to inspect it thoroughly. He removes the back cover and looks inside. As he lowers it, he rubs his chin with one hand and grips the counter with the other.

I know what he's going to say.

'Miss Prescott,' he starts slowly. 'I'm sorry. But I'm not sure this watch is worth fixing.'

I roll forward onto the balls of my feet. 'Why not?'

'Because,' Mr McCail sighs and places the pocket-watch on the counter next to him, 'in order to repair this watch, I'd need to completely replace all of the gears. Beyond that, I'd have to replace the glass on the front, repaint the face and essentially rebuild the watch from the cogs up. It would be awfully expensive to do and I truly don't think it's worth it.'

'It is!' I say without thinking. Mr McCail rubs between his eyes.

'And why would that be?' he asks.

I stop.

Suddenly I'm not really sure. I wanted the watch fixed so badly but I didn't really think about why. 'Because...'

I suppose it's because it feels wrong to let such a beautiful watch be discarded, forgotten, deemed worthless, just because it's broken. But I can't say that to Mr McCail. He'd laugh at me.

I stammer for a moment before he holds up a hand to interrupt me. 'Miss Prescott, I can't fix that watch. I can't afford to. But,' he says as I start to interrupt. 'Why don't you take it? Try and fix it yourself. I've taught you enough about clockmaking. You already know how to make gears, don't you?'

I take a deep breath. Fix the watch myself. I can do that.

I slowly nod. 'Okay. I'll try.'

Mr McCail watches me for a moment, before he holds up his index finger. 'Give me one minute,' he says, before sliding off his counter and ducking into the back of the shop. I wait, leaning against the counter and trying to peer into the shadows to see what he's doing.

He comes back, carrying with him a brown bag. It clinks as he puts it on the counter. I stand on my tiptoes, trying to see inside. 'What is it?' I ask.

Mr McCail smiles and opens the bag. Inside I can see worn tools, gears and pieces of metal all jumbled together. 'I... what?' I stammer out, staring at him.

He shrugs. 'I had some spare tools. I was planning to wait until your birthday to give these to you, but I suppose I can give them early.' He pushes the bag over to me.

I stare at him numbly. He... he's giving me tools. For my birthday. Sort of.

'Why?' I breathe out.

'Because.' Mr McCail leans against his counter and watches me through gentle eyes. 'Because you know the clocks, how they tick, how they work and move together. You know the music of clockwork and,' he smiles wryly, 'trust me, that's not a skill easily obtained.' He steps back and glances around his shop. 'I don't have the money to make you my apprentice, but I would in a heartbeat. And I think this is the next best thing.'

I try in vain to swallow past the lump in my throat and reach out for the bag, pulling it down and slinging it over my shoulder. 'Thank you,' I whisper.

Mr McCail smiles kindly and pats my hand. 'You are very welcome. Now, take your watch. I'm sure with enough work and care, it'll work well,' he tells me.

I smile back and grab the watch tightly in one hand, before waving goodbye and leaving the shop.

As I run down the cobbled street, the stones pushing through my shoes and hurting the soles of my feet, the letters slip and slide under my waistcoat. I'd almost forgotten about them, I realise. I stop and pull the new bag from my shoulder, pulling the letters out from under my waistcoat and shoving them into the bag. Nice and safe in there, hopefully.

I reach home after about ten minutes of running and skid to a halt as I stare up at the house. Me, Dad and my sister rent a room on the top floor. It's not the nicest, but the rent's cheap. I finger the shillings in my pocket as I look up at the building with its cracked shingled roof and dirt-covered red bricks.

If I go up with the shillings, the likelihood of getting anything to eat tonight won't be high. Dad'll take them and go drinking. I sigh and look around. Getting food first would probably be best. Hopefully it won't take both of the shillings. It shouldn't, at least if I get the right shop.

I set off at a run and find the nearest baker's, popping in to buy a small loaf of bread. As I wait in line, I note that it costs a shilling. The baker's eyes follow me as I move towards the counter. I just stick my hands in my pockets and grin at him. I'm not planning to steal anything and if he thinks I am, he'll just have to deal with it. I'm not going out of my way to make him comfortable.

I hand over the shilling, take the bread and run back home. I inhale slowly, before I grip the door handle tightly and head inside.

Once I reach our room, I push open the door only to be hit by the stench of alcohol and vomit. I take a few more steps into the room to see Dad sitting on the bed, a near-empty bottle of beer in his hand. Ruthie lies along the back wall, her face pale as she sleeps. I slip over to her and sit. Carefully, I put the bag down, pushing it so that it's between the pillow and the wall. Dad probably won't care about it – he doesn't care about much beyond drinking anymore – but better not to risk him wanting to sell it. I'm not sure I could bear that.

'Oi, Annie.' Dad's voice makes me jump even though I already knew he was there. 'You get any money today?'

I nod. 'Yes, sir,' I say quietly, holding out the single shilling to him. 'Two shillings. I used one to buy this bread.' I wave the loaf at him.

Dad looks at the shilling and the bread and shrugs. 'Right.' He takes the shilling and puts it in his pocket.

'How's Ruthie?' I ask, glancing back at my sister.

Dad looks up at me, his eyes bloodshot. 'She's been alright. Sleeping mostly.'

I nod, before sinking down next to her. Ruthie is, or was at least, a prostitute. She went out for the first time a year ago, after Mum died and Dad lost his job. Dad didn't know then and he doesn't know now, he still thinks she got a job as a shopgirl. In a way, that's almost true. I wanted to tell him back then, but Ruthie made me promise not to. I don't know what he'd say, but I can't imagine it'd be a pleasant reaction.

I almost broke that promise when Ruthie got hurt. I still don't know what happened. She won't talk about it, but three weeks ago she limped into the room with blood dripping down her face and a broken ankle. We had to use nearly all the money we'd saved to get her medical treatment. I didn't mention the hand-shaped bruises around her neck to Dad, instead making sure her nightdress always covered them. The doctor mostly spoke to me anyway, as Dad wasn't in any state to do it. Hiding the bruises wasn't too difficult.

I reach out and brush my hand over Ruthie's hair, curling a strand of it around my finger. Her hair is like Dad's, as black as soot from a chimney and softer than anything.

My hand drops and I turn around so that my back is to Dad, then carefully pull out the bundle of letters from the bag. I run my fingers over the yellowing paper. They look like they're a few years old, at least. The folds are deep; they look like they've been opened and reread again and again. The handwriting on the front is neat and careful. I pull out one letter as quietly as I can and turn it around to feel the pattern of the red seal.

For a moment, curiosity nearly overwhelms me. I want to open it. I want to see what's inside, what's so important about these letters that they've been kept for years, lovingly opened and folded and reopened and refolded over and over again, treated like every word is worth more than all of Buckingham Palace.

I slide the letter back into its bundle. No. If these letters mean so much to someone, it would never be right to read them. I'd hate it if someone did that to me. I have to take them back to their owner. I turn them around and look at the address again. Assuming the recipient is the owner and that the owner still lives in the same place, then I have the address. I could take them back tonight, once Dad's headed out to drink. Nobody'd even know.

There's a lot that could go wrong, I know that. I could take them back and find an empty house or a house with different occupants. The owner could accuse me of stealing them, have me arrested.

But, as I look at the lovingly folded letters, I know I can't do anything else.

I slide the bundle back under my waistcoat, standing

up to open the window slightly and let the smell out. The thick air of London rushes in to fill the room, almost choking me. I grimace. Still, it's better than trying to sleep in a room smelling like it did before. I turn around, leaning against the wall. Dad is lying back on his bed, staring at the ceiling. His eyes are red and raw. He's been crying again.

The violin case lies next to his bed, untouched.

When Mum was alive, he used to open it up and play jaunty tunes. Mum would dance, her red hair shining in the candlelight. Sometimes he'd play songs and she'd sing along, the Irish lilt to her voice making the song infinitely more beautiful. Dad'd grin widely, flick his hair back from his eyes, and sometimes he'd dance with her, still playing, the music building to a crescendo. It was moments like that when I could see why Mum married him.

But not now. After Mum's body was dragged out of the Thames, he put his violin away and hasn't taken it out since, leaving it to gather dust.

I lost two parents that day. Mum to the river, Dad to his grief.

I sink down the wall, hugging my knees to my chest, and pull the bag to me. I open it, reaching in and running my fingers over the tools, then I pull the watch out of my pocket and remove the back. I take out the tool I need and set to work.

A sound comes from beside me, startling me out of my work. Ruthie is moving, finally awake. She pushes herself up with my help, until she's settled with her back against the wall. She and I look nothing alike. I've got Mum's looks: red hair, grey eyes and so freckled that I look like someone's played darts with my face. Ruthie's as dark as Dad: black hair, brown eyes and creamy skin. Far prettier than I'll ever be.

I smile at her. 'I got some food,' I say, pulling the bread out and tearing off a piece. 'You should eat something.'

Ruthie gives the food a distasteful look. 'I'm not really hungry.'

I hold the bread out. 'Ruthie, try, please.'

She looks at me, then at the bread, then back at me. Finally, she closes her eyes and holds out her hand. I drop the bread into her palm and she starts eating it.

I sit back against the wall and watch her eat, absently pulling off a bit of the loaf for myself. The bedsprings creak as Dad stands up.

'I need some air,' he says. He doesn't need to say where he's going.

Once he's gone and the sun starts to set, Ruthie finishes eating and curls up again. After a few minutes, I pull out the bundle from my waistcoat and read the address: 45 Cranberry Street. I know where that is.

I stand up, shoving the bundle back under my waistcoat. I brush the letters through the fabric.

'Annie?' Ruthie sits up, frowning at me. 'Where are you going?'

I shrug. 'Just for a walk,' I lie.

Ruthie doesn't argue, but she doesn't stop looking

suspicious. She lies back down. Before I set off, I glance at the bag and lean forward, grabbing the watch out of it, carefully replacing the back then putting it in my pocket. I take the stairs down to the ground floor two at a time.

The smog-filled air hits me as I step outside, the low-hanging grey clouds making it even more difficult to see than it would be normally. I pull my dress sleeves down, shivering. I set off, running through the alleyways and down the lonely streets.

I leave the East End and head west towards Piccadilly. Makes sense a pair of toffs would live around there, even though they're not on the street itself. I run down the streets, searching for the sign for Cranberry Street. After about thirty minutes of running and searching, I find it. I stop where I am, staring at the sign.

This is it.

I set off at a more sedate pace, scanning the houses for number 45. Finally, I see it. Refusing to allow myself time to hesitate and ditch the whole idea, I run up to the front door. It's black, made of ebony wood, with a giant brass knocker on it in the shape of an owl. I reach out and lift it. Heavy too. I let it drop back against the door with a loud thump.

After a minute, the door opens soundlessly, revealing a tall butler with white hair, blue eyes and a bright red bow tie. I force back a laugh at the sight. 'Erm, hello,' I say, making an effort to enunciate properly. 'I'm here to see the occupants of the house.'

The butler narrows his eyes at me, almost certainly

looking at my torn, dirty brown dress and messy hair. 'Might I enquire what for?'

'I picked up something that belongs to them,' I say, suddenly self-conscious as I start to comb my hands through my curly hair, trying to making it look more presentable.

The butler does not seem impressed.

'What exactly is it that you have for them?' he asks.

I pull out the bundle. 'These letters,' I reply.

The butler's eyes widen. He shakes his head slightly and reaches out. 'I shall take them to the mistress,' he says.

I step back, clutching the bundle tightly. 'No, I'll only give them to the owners,' I insist, remembering the lovingly folded letters. I can't just hand them off to some butler. They're too precious.

The butler raises an eyebrow, before nodding. 'Only the mistress is here at the moment,' he informs me. 'She's in the drawing room. I shall speak with her and see what she wants. One moment please.'

I wait on the doorstep as he shuts the door. A few minutes pass before he opens the door again.

'The mistress would like to see you,' he says, holding the door open for me to walk through. 'Follow me.'

I follow the butler through the house, staring at the expensive decoration. The carpet is a rich red, the walls cream and gilded. Sculptures and paintings line the hallway, everything carefully designed to look as well-off as possible. Compared to my tiny room at home, it's like a palace.

I tuck my dirty hands into my pockets, scared of touching anything. I'd probably get arrested just for mucking it all up. Finally, the butler arrives at a door and knocks, stepping inside.

'The young lady here to see you, ma'am,' I hear him say. I'm a young lady now, am I? That's a first. He steps aside and gestures for me to enter.

I try to straighten my dress as I obey. The room beyond is no less lavish. A patterned yellow and green carpet covers the floor, with mahogany bookshelves lining the walls. A card table sits along the back wall, paused in the middle of a game it seems. A green sofa lies just in front of it and sitting on the sofa is a lady. The one from the carriage.

She's younger than I expected, perhaps no more than forty. Her face shows few wrinkles, despite her completely silver hair. Her dress is now black, a mourning dress. She tilts her head to the side, with creases between her eyes as she examines me.

'I hear you have something for me, child,' she says.

I step forward, instinctively fidgeting a little, reaching under my waistcoat and pulling out the bundle of letters. 'These fell out of your carriage, ma'am,' I say, holding them out to her.

Her eyes go wide and wet, her hand flying to her mouth. 'You... found them?' she chokes out. 'You really found them.'

A little taken aback by the sudden show of emotion, I nod, taking a few steps forward. 'Yes, ma'am.'

She shakes her head, rising to her feet and snatching the bundle, hugging it tightly to her chest. Tears glisten on her face. 'Thank you,' she breathes after a few minutes.

I smile nervously, reaching up to tug at my hair. 'It was really nothing, ma'am,' I say. 'I'll get out of your way.'

I turn and take a few steps towards the door, but am halted by her voice. 'Wait.'

I turn around. 'Yes, ma'am?' I ask, still ready to leave the second she gives me permission.

The woman watches me silently for a moment. 'How did you find me?' she asks quietly.

'Your address was on the front of the letters, ma'am,' I say.

She glances down at them, before looking back at me. 'You... can read?' she asks.

What sort of tom-rot is that? Just because I'm poor, doesn't mean I can't read. I don't say any of that out loud though. Instead, I draw myself up and nod. 'Yes, ma'am. My mum taught me my letters and I went on from there myself after she died.'

The woman looks at the bundle in her hands again, before raising her eyes to look at me. 'You did not read them?'

I shake my head. 'No, ma'am,' I say. 'I didn't think it'd be right to do that. They're your letters.'

She smiles slightly. 'Thank you,' she whispers.

I nod. 'That's quite alright, ma'am,' I say, stuffing my hands in my pockets without thinking about it.

A loud clink sounds as something hits the floor. I look

down and glimpse the pocket-watch. I drop to my knees, grabbing it and dusting it off. Well, at least it doesn't seem any more broken.

The sound of footsteps comes over to me and I look up to see the woman watching me.

'Is... that yours?' she asks.

I nod. 'I found it,' I say. 'I'm going to fix it up.'

She stares at me, then tilts her head to the side. 'You know how to fix clocks?'

I nod quickly. 'I work for a clockmaker. He's taught me all kinds of things.'

She raises her eyes to study the wall. She goes silent for a few minutes and I'm left at the door, staring at her. Finally, she seems to come to a decision. 'Follow me,' she says, striding forward, her skirts swishing about her ankles. 'I have something I wish to show you.'

I obey without hesitation, following her down the corridor beyond the drawing room. Through even more lavish rooms and halls we walk, until finally we reach a large, heavy oak door. The woman pushes it open, stepping aside to wave me in. She follows me and shuts the door behind us.

It's a library. Twice the height of the other rooms, with two levels of bookshelves and a balcony going around the entire room making up the second level. The bookshelves sag slightly under the weight of the books. The floor is made of rich mahogany. Two large chairs, covered in royal-blue velvet, have been arranged by the bookshelves, with a carefully engraved table between them. There's one window, hidden behind curtains in the same shade of blue.

I finally turn around.

The woman stands at the door, which is built in with a carved parapet above it, looking around the room with an expression of such grief that it nearly takes my breath away. Finally, she looks back at me. 'I haven't opened this library in so long,' she murmurs. 'Not since my son left.'

She reaches up and brushes some of the books with her fingertips, wiping away some of the dust. She takes her hand back, looking at the layer of dust on her fingers for a moment, before she strides onwards and turns around.

'Look up there.' She points behind me, above the door.

I stare at her. 'What?' I say, turning around and looking where she pointed. What might be another window hangs there, about a foot up from the parapet, covered in the same curtains as the main window. 'What's that?'

The woman carefully walks forward and reaches for a rope hanging by the door. She pulls on it and the curtains slide back, revealing the most stunning clock I have ever seen. The main body is made from gold and inlaid with different jewels: emeralds, sapphires, diamonds, rubies and quartz. The face is cream, the numbers elegantly painted on with shining golden paint. All sorts of flowers – roses, daisies, buttercups, daffodils, lilies and chrysanthemums – are painted around the numbers in circular motions, beginning at the centre and swirling outwards. The hands look like they're made of obsidian. And, the crowning glory, a painting along the base of the clock with small hinges on the left side of it. It's a picture of the woman herself, much younger with bright blonde hair and a warm smile. Beside her stands a young man with dark hair and a gentle smile and a small dark-haired boy with bright blue eyes.

'It's beautiful,' I whisper. My eyes narrow and I turn. 'Why are you showing me this?' I ask.

The woman begins to smile. 'As you can see,' she says, 'the clock does not work. I would like you to fix it. I will pay you whatever you deem appropriate.'

I stare at her, frozen in shock. 'Why?' I manage to get out. 'Why would you trust me with this?'

Her smile widens. 'You brought my letters back without opening them, without so much as asking for payment for your actions. In doing so, you have shown your honesty and kindness. What's more, you tell me you know how to fix clocks. I truly believe you would be the right person for this job.'

My hand goes to my mouth. While I know that I should be thinking about what she would pay me for this, should be thinking of feeding both me and Ruthie, thinking of paying the rent, I'm not. All I can think of is what that clock must look like on the inside, how all those gears work, how I can put them back together.

There's a silence, but neither of us break it. We don't need to. We both know what my answer will be.

After it is decided, she leads me to the back entrance, telling me to use it when I next come to the house. 'The butler will let you in if you knock,' she says. I smile and step outside into the crisp night air. 'One more thing,' she says as I walk away. I stop, turning back to her. 'My name is Elizabeth Sinclair. And you are?'

'Annie Prescott,' I say. 'My name's Annie Prescott.'

With that I leave, glancing back only once to see her standing in the doorway, surrounded by a gently glowing light.

I work on the watch during the night. The next morning, I make sure both Ruthie and Dad eat something, clean up the room, grab my bag and then head out to Cranberry Street.

It looks very different in the daytime. The houses are clean and shining in the sunlight. People wander about, with their elegant clothes and tall top hats. I make sure to duck around them all and into the alleyway leading to the back door. I knock and the butler lets me in. I smile at him as I ask to be shown to the library.

He doesn't smile in return, showing me to the library without so much as a flicker of expression. I take a minute to take in the room again, before turning to him and asking for a ladder. He brings me one and I set to work.

I climb up the ladder and perch on the top of the parapet above the doorframe, stealing a moment to brush my fingers over the beautiful clock. Then I grab a cloth and start cleaning it.

With each wipe of the cloth revealing more of the stunning clock beneath dust, I begin to appreciate more and more the skill of whoever made it. I then set to work restoring the clock face. For the most part, it's intact, but there are small parts that need to be repainted. Each touch of the brush makes anxiety build up in me. I can't ruin this clock. I just can't.

I finish restoring the face, then kneel down so I can more easily reach the base where the painting door is. I manage to open it and get a good look at the mechanism inside. The clock's beauty continues within. Each gear is carefully crafted and perfectly arranged so that the clock keeps time. At first, I can't see anything wrong with it. The gears seem to all be in place and they certainly don't appear to be rusty or broken. Then I spot it. High up, one of the gears has broken, snapped clean in half. It's not a big gear, not at all. In fact, in the grand scheme of things it might not be thought to be at all important. But that is the only thing keeping the clock from working.

I climb down the ladder and drop to the dusty floor, then I pull open my bag and search through it. There's no gear the right size. I'll have to make a new one.

It's not like I haven't made gears before and they don't take that long, but the consequences of making a mistake have never been so high. What if I hurt the clock more by trying?

I take a deep breath and gather myself. I can do this.

I take out a piece of metal and the other equipment I need and set to work.

After hours of labour, I hold up a perfectly formed gear. It's not as stunning as the other gears inside the clock; it almost feels like desecration to put a gear as mundane as this in there. But I have to fix it.

I climb up the ladder and peer inside the clock, before reaching up and removing the broken gear. In goes the new, softly clicking into place. I quickly oil all of the gears, before I move back.

I find the wind-up key just below the clock and quickly check the mainspring inside before I turn it. Around and around I go, then I release it.

And the clock starts.

I sit back on the parapet, balancing carefully, and stare at it for a few minutes, the tick-tock softly chattering away.

There is nothing in the world quite like the sound of a clock.

But the room is too dark to see it properly. I shimmy down the ladder, running to the window where I pull open the royal-blue curtains. Dust hits me in the face and I cough, wincing. The windowsill has been painted a creamy colour, but dust covers it. A single vase of wilting forget-me-nots stands in the centre.

I run to the door and find the butler, asking him to bring me some cleaning supplies. Once he gives them to me, I pull out a duster and set to work, carefully wiping around the vase. I touch the flowers with a careful fingertip, before tying back the curtains and starting to clean the window itself.

Afterwards, I pull myself to my feet, light the oil lamps and look around. It's finished.

A chime makes me jump and I spin, staring at the clock. The hands have hit five o'clock and five loud, pure chimes echo throughout the house.

One. Two. Three. Four. Five.

A gasp comes from the doorway. Mrs Sinclair stands there, staring at the room. I bite my lip, my hands behind my back. 'I'm sorry if you didn't want me to clean up,' I say. 'I just thought the room could use more light; the clock looks better in the light.'

She shakes her head, stumbling forward. 'It's... quite alright,' she whispers, before she turns and catches sight of the clock. Her face pales.

Silence.

'Mrs Sinclair?' I ask nervously, trying to interpret her reaction. 'Is it alright?'

She looks at me with wide shining eyes. 'It's not just alright. It's perfect,' she chokes out, before starting to cry.

I hurry forward, my hand reaching out to touch her shoulder. I hesitate. Would a rich lady want me to touch her? Particularly when I've been messing around with gears and oils.

Then she lets out a sob and I realise that I don't give a fig. I press my hand tightly into her shoulder.

At first, she stiffens, then she practically collapses to the ground, pressing her face to her hands. Sobs shake her whole body. 'Thank you,' she manages to say. 'Th-thank you so much.'

I drop to my knees next to her, keeping my hand on her shoulder. I'm not sure how long we sit there for, but finally she stops crying and pulls away. She doesn't look nearly so regal as she did before, with her face red and blotchy. I reckon she looks better this way. More human.

She stares up at the ticking clock again, before she looks back at me. 'You... can read, correct?'

I blink. 'Yes, ma'am,' I say, tilting my head in confusion.

'How would you like to read one of these books to me?' she asks quietly.

My eyes light up. 'Oh, very much, ma'am,' I say.

Her smile widens. 'Choose a book then, Annie,' she says, walking forward to take a seat.

I choose a book, *Pride and Prejudice* by Jane Austen, and take the other chair. I start to read out loud, trying my best to read clearly. Time passes quickly and before I know it, it's time to go home.

Mrs Sinclair gives me the money for the clock, a whole thirty shillings. 'Come back when you want,' she tells me. 'I'd love to have you read to me again.'

I smile at her and nod.

I leave, hurrying home, pausing to buy some food along the way, and I give Dad the remaining money when I arrive. He takes it, narrowing his eyes at me. 'Where've you been?' he asks, glancing at the coins.

I bite my lip. 'I've got a job,' I say.

'With who?' he asks.

'With this rich lady,' I say. 'I fixed her clock and now she's letting me read to her.'

Dad watches me for a minute, before shrugging and leaving the room. I give Ruthie something to eat and then go to sleep.

And that is how it continues for several months. I start out for Cranberry Street and spend the day reading to Mrs Sinclair, in that beautiful room, with that beautiful clock. The tick-tocking fills the air and makes me feel happier than any of the books or any of the money. She pays me at the end; somehow I feel like I might have become her companion or something like that. Then I hurry home, making sure Ruthie eats.

One day, I'm reading the *Iliad* to Mrs Sinclair, curled up on one of the velvet chairs and frowning at the complex poetry. Every so often, she jumps in to help me with a word. She's been silent for a few minutes by this point and I start to come to the end of a chapter.

'My son and I used to do this,' Mrs Sinclair says, so softly that I almost don't hear.

I stop and look at her. 'Do what?' I ask.

She doesn't look at me, just stares entranced at the bookshelves. 'Sit in here, reading books,' she says. 'He'd curl up next to me and we'd read through them together. My husband doesn't come in here, you see. It was our safe place. But,' her eyes grow wet and she bites her lip, 'but then he got into a fight with his father and left. Now he's gone.'

Somehow, I didn't think she just meant gone from the house. 'What happened to him?' I ask gently.

She glances at me. 'He died,' she says in a monotone. 'Fell into the Thames and drowned.'

She falls silent for a moment and I stay quiet too, running my fingers over the pages of the book. Waiting.

'That's what my husband and I were doing in the East End that day you found my letters,' she starts again. 'His landlady told us that he had had a dalliance with a young woman there and we had discovered her identity.' She shakes her head. 'My husband was hoping to pay her off, make sure she'd never tell anyone about him, never tell anyone how he had... disgraced us.' Her voice takes on a tone of disgust at the word 'disgraced.' 'I took a different tack. I only wish...' She stops for a moment, looking past me as though she's seeing someone behind me. I glance behind only to see empty space. Mrs Sinclair continues on, speaking as though she's in a dream, 'Those letters were from him, you know, from my son. Ever since he died, I haven't been able to let them out of my sight. When they fell from my carriage... well.' She shakes her head again, pulling herself out of her state. 'Well, I couldn't...'

I stay silent, absently brushing the words on the page with my fingertips. 'You must miss him a lot,' I say after a while.

'Very much.'

I stare at the floor, before I speak again. 'My mum died in the river too.'

She looks at me, her eyes wide. 'What?'

'She jumped though,' I say. 'Couldn't stand living anymore.'

Mrs Sinclair presses her hand tightly into my shoulder. Comforting and strong.

'That's my son,' she says, gesturing to the painting below the clock. I look closely at the small boy with the wide smile.

I pause to blink back tears and return to reading the book aloud.

I go home with the money she's paid me and hand it to Dad. I make sure Ruthie eats and curl up in the back of the room, intermittently napping and working on the watch, thinking of that boy in the picture and Mum all the while.

On my next visit I step inside the door, smiling at the butler, who now smiles back. I follow the familiar path to the library, pushing open the door to find Mrs Sinclair already inside. We both sit in our chairs and I take the *Iliad* up once more, starting to read it aloud. Soon I am engrossed in the story of Troy. I'm so engrossed, in fact, that I jump violently when the door swings open.

I barely have time to notice that Mrs Sinclair has gone ashen, before a man strides inside. A very familiar man, even though I've only seen him once. In the carriage with Mrs Sinclair, shoving a boy to the ground.

'Elizabeth, what...' he starts, glaring at his wife, before he catches sight of me and his eyes go even harder. 'Who is *that*?'

I shrink back against the chair. Mrs Sinclair stands up. 'I hired her,' she says quickly. 'To clean up the library and read to me. Don't hurt her, Aaron. It's not her fault.'

The man, presumably Mr Sinclair, sends her a dark look. 'You hired the scum of the street,' he snarls. 'To work in *my* house?'

I look desperately towards Mrs Sinclair, who steps in front of me. 'She is not scum,' she says. 'She brought my letters back...'

'Those letters! Even after death must that boy cause us problems?' He turns on me, his eyes cold. 'Get out of my house.'

I jump to my feet, dropping the book on the chair. 'Yes, sir,' I say, my legs shaking.

'Aaron.' Mrs Sinclair steps forward, her hand outstretched. 'Please...'

Mr Sinclair slaps her hand away, sending her stumbling backwards. 'Don't talk to me,' he says coldly. 'I'll deal with you later. You,' he looks towards me. 'Get out.'

I nod hurriedly, glancing towards Mrs Sinclair, who looks at me with sad eyes. I back away and hurry from the room. Shouting erupts from the library and I rush to the back door, bursting out into the alleyway.

Once I'm outside, I drop against the wall, shaking violently, my legs unable to hold me. I suck in air, trying to calm down. Nausea builds up in my throat and I choke back a sob, falling to my knees, my hand at my mouth. If that was what Mr Sinclair had always been like, no wonder his son left.

I close my eyes, feeling my breath finally coming somewhat slower and the nausea fading a little. Finally, I push myself to my feet and stumble away.

I find my way home and step inside, staring dully around. The small room, with its brown walls and floor and tiny window, seems so much more confining. I sit down next to Ruthie.

'Annie?' Ruthie asks.

I don't answer. I can't.

Ruthie tries a few more times to get my attention, before dropping it. Dad rolls over to stare at me.

'What's the matter?' he asks.

I don't say anything and faintly I hear Ruthie answer. I don't hear what she says.

I can't do this. I can't be here.

I shove myself to my feet and run from the room, shrugging off Ruthie's hand as I do so. I run out of the house, down the street and away, away. My feet wander without my direction, leading me to Mr McCail's.

I stare up at the sign, before I stumble inside and slip behind the counter. The room beyond has clocks hanging from the ceiling, from the walls and even lying on the floor. It's a tick-tocking paradise.

I drop and hug my knees to my chest, closing my eyes. Listening to the tick-tock and imagining every problem flying away each time it ticks. Tick. There goes Mr Sinclair's anger. Tock. There goes losing the library. Tick. There goes Ruthie's injuries. Tock. There goes Dad's drinking and grief. Tick. There goes the lack of food and money. Tock. There goes Mum's death.

The image of her body, logged and swollen with water, her eyes wide open, floods to mind and I press my face into my knees, trying to push it away.

I hope she didn't feel too much pain.

'Annie?' Mr McCail's voice startles me and I press my face more firmly into my knees. 'Annie, what's wrong?'

There's a moment of silence. 'I miss Mum,' I choke out.

Arms wrap tightly around me and it breaks away the last of my defences. I start to sob, painful, heaving sobs that don't stop coming. He begins to rock me back and forth, whispering soothing words.

Finally, the tears stop coming.

'Why did she go?' I whisper into his shoulder.

Silence.

'I don't know,' he says at last. The words fall like stones and the world is left heavier because of them.

Mr McCail helps me to my feet and we work on clocks. For hours we work, and by the time I'm finished, I feel steadier than I have for a while.

I leave as the day grows dark and reach my home in pitch-black night. I climb the steps, reaching the door and pushing it open. The room smells strongly of alcohol when I walk inside, hitting me like a train. I carefully close the door behind me.

Something is wrong.

'Dad?' I say, scanning the room for him, quietening my nerves. He's fine, he's fine. Ruthie lies sleeping along the back wall. She wouldn't be sleeping if something had—

'Annie,' Dad's voice comes from by the bed. It's a choked noise, closer to a sob than an actual word. 'There you are.'

He sounds relieved.

I stumble forward, frowning as I finally catch sight of him. For some reason, perhaps a vain attempt to hide from everything and everyone, he's behind his bed. It's been pushed out by a couple of feet so that he can fit and now his face peers over it. It's puffy and not just from alcohol. 'Dad, what's wrong?'

He stares up at me. 'Where have you been?' he hisses, forcing himself to his feet and clambering over the mattress, coming to stand in front of me. 'I... Where did you go?' The words are snarled out, false-angry. He's not angry. Why...?

Then it hits me. He thought I'd...

'Dad, I just needed some time alone,' I say. 'I'm sorry. I didn't mean to make you worried.'

Dad stares at me, before he drops down onto his bed. 'I thought you'd gone away,' he whimpers. 'Like she did.'

I sit down next to him. 'I'm not going anywhere,' I say quietly.

He looks at me, before his face crumples and he starts to cry. I reach out and hug him tightly. 'Why did she go?' he sobs. 'Why did she leave me?'

I don't answer. I can't.

I hear Ruthie shift and murmur a question, wondering what's going on, but I can't answer her. Somehow, I know that if I turn away now, Dad will go away again and this time he won't be coming back.

'Do you remember when we used to dance?' Dad whispers through his tears.

I nod. 'You used to dance all around the room,' I say. 'Seconds later you'd be screaming at each other over something though.' I laugh a little. 'Then you'd end up kissing, gripping each other with white knuckles, like...' My laugh trails off. 'Like it was the only thing keeping you alive.'

Dad stays silent for a moment. 'I felt alive,' he admits. 'She... When we fought, when we danced, when we kissed, I felt alive. In a way that... only she could ever manage.' His voice breaks. 'When I met her, I was just an urchin. Nobody really. She was... a dancer, a musician. She was so beautiful, twirling in the air, her red hair flying around her. And kind. She was so kind. Untouched, somehow, by our world.' He smiles faintly. 'I thought she was an angel.'

I take hold of his hand tightly.

'When she started to go downhill,' he begins. 'When she started to burst into tears at nothing and lie in bed for hours at a time, her eyes empty...' His voice sounds wet through the darkness. 'I tried everything to help her.' He lets out a broken laugh. 'I played my violin next to her bed, trying to get her to dance with me. Like if she'd just get up and dance, maybe she could go back to being my angel again. Untouched. But no.

'Then I thought I could go out and buy her things, buy her back to herself.' He shook his head. 'It seems foolish now. But I was getting desperate. I bought her favourite foods, a pretty dress. Anything to get her to react. At first, she did. Then she didn't.'

I slip my arm around his shoulder, gripping him tightly. I remember this. By that point, Dad started to give up hope. He stopped trying to get her to do anything. When he wasn't working, he'd just lie next to her, holding her.

'When she died,' Dad whispers, 'I lost more than just...'

He doesn't finish, his voice trailing off, the words left twisting in the air. I close my eyes and lean against his shoulder.

'She was my everything.' His voice shatters like a broken clock. 'I... can't do this without her.'

He starts to sob again, collapsing into broken cries. He cries for so long that his sobs become voiceless, his throat hoarse. He stops and pulls away from me, staring emptily at the opposite wall.

The sight is so familiar. Painfully familiar. That look...

I glance at Ruthie, who's watching us through half-closed eyes, then back at Dad. No. I can't let this happen.

I stand up and kneel down by the violin case. Reaching inside, I pull out the violin and put it up to my shoulder. I can vaguely remember some of Dad's old lessons. I was never the best student, but I can play a few tunes.

It takes me a moment to summon up all of my courage, then I start to play Psalm 23. It was Mum's favourite.

The tune is croaky, weak, but recognisable. I see Dad's eyes flicker and he looks at me like I'm a stranger.

I ignore it and carry on playing until I reach the end. I lower my arms, still holding onto the violin and bow.

Dad's eyes are more alert than I've seen them in a long time. He shakes his head at me. 'Annie, that's not how you hold the bow,' he scolds me, standing up and pushing me into the right position.

By the time Ruthie manages to summon up the energy to drag herself over to us, Dad's engrossed in telling me where exactly I went wrong and I'm engrossed in listening to him. We talk for so long that our voices go hoarse, and after hours of it, I wander back to my pillow and start to work on my watch, listening as he and Ruthie chatter away. Then, when Ruthie lies down next to me, I put the watch down, curl up and fall asleep with her hugging me and music in my ears.

I awaken in the morning to the sound of carriage wheels outside my window. I frown and roll over, carefully slipping out of Ruthie's grip. The sun is already high in the sky; I've slept in far later than I usually do. I stand up and lean outside, craning my neck to look down at the street below. My eyes widen as they catch sight of the Sinclair carriage and I run from the room, taking the stairs two steps at a time. I come out of the house, slowing to a walk and finally stopping next to the carriage.

Mrs Sinclair steps out, alone it seems. Her face is pale and she's shaking slightly, but as the late-morning sun hits her face I see her relax. She catches sight of me and immediately looks relieved. 'Annie, there you are. I've been looking for you, asking around the East End. I... I'm sorry about my husband,' she says. 'He can be... difficult, sometimes.'

I don't say anything, simply watch her with careful eyes. She bites her lip and casts her eyes back at the carriage, before looking back at me. 'I brought you something,' she says, reaching inside the carriage and bringing out two things. The first, a purse of money, more than she's ever given me before from the weight of it. The second, a book: the *Iliad*.

I take them both, staring at her. 'What...?'

'You didn't get to finish the book,' she says, staring at the clouds with a wistful expression. 'And I think our time in the library will have to come to an end. My husband will not allow it anymore. He does not know I am here, but I could not leave you without payment and without finishing that book,' she smiles with damp eyes. 'Thank you.'

'What for?' I ask.

'For everything.' She looks up at the house, as the sunrays brush her face. 'I haven't been outside like this in such a long time.'

I smile. 'You should do it more often,' I tell her.

Her gaze drops to me. 'Perhaps I shall.'

She turns and climbs back into the carriage, which starts off.

I watch after her, even after she turns the corner and is gone from my sight. Finally, my gaze drops to the purse of money. There's enough here to pay the rent for several months in a better place than we have been living, even with food. I look up again at the street where she had stood, a smile on my face.

Turning around, I walk back to the house and climb the stairs, pushing open the door and stepping inside.

Both Ruthie and Dad look up as I come back. I drop the bag of money on the floor. 'I just got paid,' I say.

Both of them stare at me, then at the money, then back at me. 'All of that?' Ruthie whispers.

I nod, my smile widening. 'There's enough there for rent, right?'

Ruthie pulls herself forward and searches through the bag. 'Oh yes,' she says, looking up at me. 'There's more than enough.'

'Maybe we'll have enough for a proper Christmas meal this year,' I say.

Ruthie grins back, her eyes alight.

Dad coughs and pushes himself to his feet. For a moment, both me and Ruthie stare at him. Then he strides over to his violin case and pulls out the instrument. 'I think this calls for a song,' he says, turning to smile at us. He starts to play a jolly tune that I remember him and Mum dancing to. Ruthie bursts out laughing and starts to clap along.

The music fills our little room and makes it seem infinite. I smile, watching as Dad begins to dance.

I sit down by my pillow, glancing at where I left the watch. And, as I look at it, I hear it start to tick.

THE BEACH HOUSE

LUKE MATTHEWS

I'm thirty tomorrow and my life already feels like it's over.

I guess you might wonder why I'd say something like that. My name's Nick by the way, or Nicky, or sometimes even Nicholas. It kind of depends who's saying it and why, you know? Why would somebody like me feel their life's already over? Well, that's kind of a story in itself.

It'd be good to show you around my house. Don't worry, it's not a sales pitch. I couldn't leave this place if I wanted to. I guess it's pride as much as anything else, wanting to show it off.

I love this house. It's by the beach. I built it myself, mostly anyway. I mean, I had a little help. It was abandoned when I got here, neglected and rotting away. Seriously. Can you believe it? I needed a home and it just needed some love, that's all, so it was a perfect fit, I guess.

I have a memory of this house from so long ago that I can't even say for sure if it's real or not. Me and Nat – that's Natalie, my twin sister – playing here, sitting on the beach near this place and playing together, playing pretend at 'house' even at four or six years old or something.

That's what Mum says we were doing and I guess I can't even say for sure that it's definitely something I remember, if you know what I mean. I'm so young it might be that I just remember seeing the photo of it, being shown it when I was older and having it around as I was growing up.

It was certainly one of Mum's favourite photos. I know that for sure. She even had a copy made, small enough to put in a locket that she wore around her neck. She had it on the last time I saw her. At her funeral, I mean, laid in the casket. I saw the locket on her.

I wanted to reach out and take it, it felt so special and important. I wanted to take it and keep it, hold onto it forever, but I know that would've been wrong. How could I have done that at a funeral, even if she was my mother?

She looked peaceful anyway, really peaceful, like she was sleeping and maybe having a nice dream she didn't want to wake up from.

She was mine and Natalie's mother who loved us and we never doubted it, not for a second, and we loved her too. I know I did. Strange to think how it was for us once, both together inside her, before we can even remember.

I wonder how she felt hearing she'd be having twins.

You know how rare it is to have a boy and a girl together? Rare to have twins in the first place, and rarer to have identical twins, but even rarer still, and much rarer, they said, for it to be a boy and a girl. I don't know why exactly, but I do know how special it felt that we were always together, me and Natalie.

I can't say we were always happy as a family. That would be a lie. Maybe no family is, but still, I mean maybe we were unhappier than normal. I hope that doesn't sound like self-pity. We all have at least our fair share of suffering. It's how we handle it, I think – that's what makes us who we are.

It's strange looking back now as an adult. I have to accept I'm an adult now, nearly thirty, and I've done enough to say I am too. I built this house for one thing. I already mentioned that, didn't I?

I guess I can see that I wasn't perfect. Nobody is, are they? That's what they say, even if they try to be, or pretend they are. I guess it's true what it says in the Bible, how important it is to forgive and forgive and just forgive.

You'd like it if you were here, I'm sure. I don't see how anybody could want to be anywhere else except for right by the sea. Do you know how it feels, just watching the waters rolling in? All morning, all evening, just seeing it, the waves rolling in to roll back out again... only to roll back in again and back out. I'm sure you get the idea. But I could stay here for hours just watching. It's always the same in a way but each time it's kind of different too. Like how they say you never cross the same river twice?

I still can't quite describe how it makes me feel after all these years. I always wanted to be by the sea.

So listen. Maybe it's shocking – I know it must be, but I'll just come out and say it: I killed my father. There's a confession already. I did it here, right on the beach near my house, and eventually his body ended up far out at sea, deep at the bottom, to go soft in the water and feed fish, or who knows what.

That's shocking, isn't it. Should I ask for forgiveness?

Who are you, really, to forgive me anyway? If you understood, maybe you wouldn't judge me. Maybe it was a mistake. But I can't say I wouldn't do it exactly the same all over again, and so how can I say I truly regret it? Maybe if you understood – if you knew what it was like for us... Maybe I could try to tell you, if you've got time to listen.

This is how it was: me and Nat together. Along with Mum and Dad that was our whole family, the four of us. Anyway, imagine me and Natalie lying together. So young, just children, still sharing the same bed, going to sleep in the early night, slipping into sleep cuddled up together in our own room, peacefully drifting off together in the warmth like we were already in a dream, like how being a child can be for almost anybody I'm sure, and Mum comes into our room all of a sudden. I was awake enough to respond, but Nat didn't do anything more than fidget in her sleep, if that.

I remember seeing the cold look on our mum's face, pale and white like she was sick or had seen something that had put the fear into her enough to chill her blood. I must've been seven or so but I can still see it as clearly as if it was happening right now.

I can still see Mum in her make-up and remember the scent of her perfume. An overpowering smell, it mostly just stank of alcohol to me – I guess she always wore too much when she bothered to wear any at all – and she came to us quietly to pick us up. It was a struggle to lift both of us, too much, so she picked up Natalie, who still seemed more than half asleep, and held my hand and shushed me as I came round. 'Shush now, Nicky, don't make a sound. Don't ask why, just do it and come along...'

And I trusted her of course, and I did what she said, sneaking out of the house past my dad, who was drowsy in front of the blaring television, Nat turning in her sleep but not really waking up, burying her face in Mum's chest.

Out of the house and into the cold of the night in the street, the chill rolling in as Mum opened the door, Nat wincing awake as she clung, and me shivering so suddenly in my night clothes, out there at that odd hour, wondering what was going on, but either too tired or surprised or young to even ask.

Mum still trying to be quiet, unlocking the car, looking nervously behind to see if Dad had noticed. She lowered Nat quietly, gently, into the back. Nat stared up at Mum with the kind of angry face people make when sleep still has a hold on them before lying down on the seat, and she was back to sleep again already, a little scowl but eyes firmly closed, curling against the upholstery.

Mum got in the driver's seat and opened the passenger side for me. I felt so small as I got in and sat there in the front, not properly able to look out of the windscreen. I was well awake by then and really wondering what was going on. I looked over at Mum. I can remember it so clearly still, even now after all these years. I can't imagine I'll ever forget. Her skin was already pale – Mum was practically anaemic, like me – but she was gripping the steering wheel so hard, even still just parked in the driveway there, that her hands were white beyond white, translucent, with bulges of veins visible beneath skin stretched tight as she strained.

She was shaking and I don't know if I was really able to grasp it back then. Surely not, at that age; it would've all just seemed overwhelming and baffling. Looking back now, I know how worried and scared and lost she must've been – petrified – and I can see it in her now, even without her here I can see it playing in my mind.

I was staring up at her from the passenger seat and she turned to me. There were tears just beginning to form, fluid welling up around the edges of her eyes, but she bit it back and she smiled this huge smile, as though to reassure me and tell me everything's fine, there's nothing wrong, there's nothing to worry about, and she asked me – I remember it so clearly – 'Where should we go?'

Looking down at me, waiting for an answer, like I'd know, or expecting me to want to be taken somewhere – maybe somewhere fun – in the dark on a Tuesday, as a seven-year-old. I don't know, I just remember knowing it was a Tuesday because as I was falling asleep I was reminding myself to take my recorder to school tomorrow, and that was still one of the main thoughts floating around in my sleep-fogged head as I continued looking up at her, not knowing what to say.

She spoke again, sharper this time. 'Nicky. Where should we go?' I remember seeing my dad appearing out of the house, coming over to us, trying to open the locked door and leaning against the window, asking my mum what she thought she was doing.

Mum went stiff and turned round to look at him but not all the way, only halfway, like she was looking out of the front of the car, her whole body frozen and stiff, staring straight forward like he wasn't there, like she could will him out of existence just by pretending she couldn't see or hear him.

And I remember looking and seeing her hand, shaking and trembling so much now, fumbling the key into the slot with a neat little click and turning it, and as the engine ignited into life with a throaty roar my dad starting to get mad.

He had to shout now to be heard, and he was, he was shouting, calling her crazy and asking what the hell she thought she was doing, his whole face in the car window like the frame of a television, our dad, this angry head, hissing and mean and spitting out words at us in the car, engine on, still not moving.

He pounded against the window, the soft meaty thumps dull against the glass. I don't think he was trying to break it really. He was big and worked in construction. He saw he'd got my attention and tried a new tactic. 'Come on, Nicky, unlock the door...'

I froze. I didn't know what to do. I looked around the car and saw Natalie sitting bolt upright in the back. I can still see the expression on her face, mirroring my own feelings exactly, the panic and confusion, desperate to do something but not knowing what, not knowing what was the right thing to do, just a child, just wanting to cry.

Dad was still shouting at me. Mum turned again, staring at me like none of it was going on. 'Where should we go, Nicholas?' She never called me Nicholas unless I was in trouble or it was something really important. I remember being aware of lights turning on around us, neighbours curious or alarmed about the commotion.

Looking back I still can't stand the thought of it, other people suddenly intruding into our little madness. We were so vulnerable and ashamed – who were they to suddenly be there and witness it? I wanted to cry. I wanted to scream. I wanted to go back to bed and pull the sheets over me and rock until everything was better again and I could come out of the darkness knowing what to do.

I was still frozen. Mum was waiting for an answer. She looked at the road and the car started rolling forward anyway, just starting to slowly glide out of the drive. Dad was jogging sideways, his face by the back window, a mask of disbelief. I remember seeing Natalie turn to look at him. He was pleading with her; I couldn't hear the words but I know what he must've been saying. 'Come on, Nat, unlock the door, there's a good girl...'

She did. She pulled up the lever and it opened and

everything happened at once: Dad reaching in and unlocking the front door, Mum's scared look at his intrusion, her face a gasp, more cold air from outside washing in alongside a sudden hot gush of alcohol – Dad drank pretty much every night – Nat backing away, sliding across the back seat.

The car stopped. Dad was furious, berating Mum. He came in through the rear door and grabbed her hair with one hand. I remember seeing her twisting, pulling back as he hissed at her, asking her what she was playing at.

That's how it was for us sometimes, growing up. Dad just had a nasty streak. It wasn't all the time. It was just that sometimes he'd get mad about something and she'd have to watch herself, because if she pushed it or did the wrong thing he'd end up taking it out on her.

I remember how it was being a little older, trying to understand the world around me and feeling like it was so wrong that it hurt. It hurt me inside when Dad treated Mum like that, but that frustration – of not knowing what to do – what was the solution?

Then I'd come home to see Mum and Dad on the sofa together watching TV, her hands on his chest, and me just standing there staring, thinking about it, wondering how she could do that and be there with him like that, and then her looking at me. 'What's wrong, Nicky?'

I didn't have an answer, but it made me feel so wound up inside and madder than I could say.

'Go upstairs with your sister.' My mum's concerned face, her hands over his chest, like she was groping him unnoticed while he sipped a beer and seemed more interested in sport or advertising or whatever it was; I don't think it mattered as long as it was television.

I hated them both then, him for doing it and her for being weak enough to take it, but what could I do? I went upstairs to Nat. Nat was always there for me, and I knew she understood. We were always together and losing her would be like losing a piece of myself.

So maybe you can see a little bit how it was for me, for both of us, me and Nat. I mean, it's obvious Mum was unhappy, and not hard to figure out why and – well, I don't even want to tell you this – but there's something else too.

There was a time – a few times – when we were still young but older, must've been eleven or twelve – Mum would be saying goodnight to us, but it was weird, saying how much she loved us and if anything happened to her, we must know that, she wanted us to know.

Saying that, putting us to bed, still children – it made us worry. It made me worry, anyway, and one time I got out of bed after Mum left, and followed her, quietly. She'd gone to their bedroom – it still seemed strange to go into an adult's bedroom – and I was watching her sitting on the bed. There was the faraway noise from the television downstairs, stern voices, advertising jingles, maybe some explosions.

I stood in the doorway as Mum sat on the bed. She was holding a bottle of pills. We knew about them, the doctor gave them to her, she needed them as they helped with her insomnia. It sounded horrible the way she described it: a twilight desert, like a limbo she was stuck in alone, in these numb hours trapped away from reality and people, frozen in her own thoughts.

It had made me start to sleep badly, thinking about it and worrying, and I asked about the pills, but Mum had smiled and said they were far too strong for children and a child like me shouldn't need medication like that and that I should just stop worrying.

She was counting out the pills, lots of them, into her hand, slowly, more and more, then just sitting there looking at them, looking very intently like she was weighing something up, lost in thought.

After a long while she looked up and saw me reflected in the doorway in her dresser mirror. She turned to me, smiling, saying she hadn't seen us two there and asking what was up.

I remember that. She hadn't seen us two. Just like I'd been lost watching Mum, I hadn't seen Nat creep up too. She must've been behind me. She ran in and went straight to Mum and hugged her.

'Don't ever leave us, Mummy.'

Nat said it. I wanted to but I couldn't bring myself to do it. Nat was crying and nobody had to say why. Mum looked a bit teary too as she hugged her back, not properly, just a little bit of sniffling. I remember thinking twelve was too old to be saying 'Mummy' but I went and joined in the hug with Nat, whispering in Mum's ear I didn't want her to go anywhere.

She laughed. It seemed genuine when she laughed or smiled with me and my sister. She said she wasn't going anywhere and that we just needed to stop worrying. She said she couldn't leave us, she needed to stay and see us grow up.

I remember that's how she phrased it, and she was telling us how much she loved us and how special and precious we both were and I remember asking her, 'Do you love Dad, Mum?'

Mum looked sad and said life can get complicated when you're an adult, but that if you find special people, that's worth anything in the world, anything and everything, and if you do then you're lucky, probably luckier than you'll ever know.

She told us that if you're lucky like that, you have to let them know how you feel, and hold onto them. Then she said she thought both of us were special, but that it was already past our bedtimes and we knew it, creeping around still awake so late.

I knew that she meant it, about somebody special I mean, and I really took that to heart. If there's somebody like that in your life, you put them first, over and above everything and anybody else, no matter what the cost, and no matter what the world thinks and what people say. It's just too important.

If you're lucky enough to find somebody like that – and I'm not sure how many people do, maybe not that many at all – then it's the most important thing.

I remember the years between that – between really

feeling Mum's unhappiness – and the time after she was gone, and at least one time all of us trying to get away, going to the beach, to a special place. That was where the beach house was of course, where the photo had been taken when we were young.

I'm sure you wouldn't think too much of it if you saw it then, just a crumbling relic of a place, nothing special to look at unless you particularly had an interest in tumbledown things and the effect of neglect on basic materials.

It was so secluded, on a strip of coast surrounded by steep drifts of soft sand forming mounds, reed patches clumping up dotted here and there, and the sand gradually sloping down into the shoreline as the sea lapped up, eating into it.

You didn't have to go far from the road before the dunes made you feel swallowed up almost, into a blizzard of sand, a little warm oblivion of melting nothingness. That's how it seemed in my head anyway. It was exactly like every place along that shoreline for as far as you'd want to walk in either direction, I'd say, and I'd say that it was nice.

It was nice.

Out there it was a little like the rest of the world didn't matter or exist anymore, at least for a while – and isn't that what holidays are about?

It made me almost think that we could be a real family, a happy one, like just being there made everything else melt away, just for a while.

That was hard to keep up though. I remember looking at my dad, trousers rolled up over his knees, complaining about sunstroke as his skin quickly turned lobster red, the wind taking the heat of the sun away so he didn't notice until it was too late.

He was so awkward and ridiculous. I just wished he wasn't there so much. Is it wrong, to hope against hope that somebody could just be wiped away completely... written out of all history? Can we help the way we feel? When did this sadness and pain begin eating into everything? Who was I supposed to turn to?

I could tell Nat about it, even if maybe I didn't make clear how vicious my thoughts were sometimes. She'd soothe me. She was always like that, mellow and a calming influence. I don't know where I'd be without my twin. Maybe the loneliest person on the planet. The loneliest person in all history.

We'd manage to get away off on our own sometimes, saying we still felt like walking a while when Mum and Dad felt tired or found a nice place and wanted to stop for a bit and just enjoy it.

Out together amongst the dunes, just us two, me and my twin – that felt like freedom and I was happy. We were happy together as twins. That was all it took for me.

I don't know, all teenagers hate their parents, don't they? That's normal, isn't it? Well, maybe not hate, maybe that's too strong a word. I was just happy with Nat, anyway, but those times were brief and seemed lightweight and fluffy, disintegrating amongst the gruelling reality of the boredom and frustration of school and chores, the resignation to the whole thing, the smouldering resentment. Inside I felt as though something was festering.

Then Mum left.

Mum left like she'd said she would. That's how I take it: she left when we were old enough to look after ourselves. It got worse then, but I knew we couldn't go with her. She needed to be free. I understood that even then, when we were... I'm not sure; fifteen or sixteen, teenagers anyway. That was how I felt. She didn't abandon us – she escaped. She was free. If anything, I was jealous, not angry but envious of her, and desperate to do the same myself.

Questions rang in my head sometimes, they still do. Questions about how she could do this to us, or whether she thought she was the only one suffering. Mostly though – and maybe it sounds strange – I think that I was just so lucky having such a perfect mother, for as long as she was around, and I just hope she knew that.

Mum had to escape, but with just us and Dad I couldn't stand it anymore. I couldn't stand being around him. It was all his fault and he was such a slob now without Mum to pick up after him. The house got into a mess and he was too lazy to do anything after work except drink himself to sleep in front of the television.

I couldn't stand it when he tried to tell me to do anything. I had to get out of there. I needed money and so I skipped school trying to get whatever work I could; odd jobs, anything.

A letter came from the school and that was the final straw. Dad shouted at me but I wasn't going to listen to him. I stopped going home and started making friends just to crash on their couches.

I don't know if I can say why, really, but I felt that I had to go somewhere fresh. That I had to be in a different place, and all that I could think of was the town we used to go through. It was the last place with any shops or anything near the seaside. Where the beach is, and my house now.

It was a way away that town, like an hour or more after I figured it out on the train, and then you have to take the bus for a while too. It's kind of a tourist trap but the beach is only a few stops away on the bus again, like ten or fifteen minutes – well, maybe twenty – or you can walk it easily if you feel up to it. The beach is worth it. Then of course there's where I live. That's just down the beach too.

I think whoever built it in the first place must've been thinking like me, about having somewhere nice but out of the way. Whatever happened or why it got left to slip into such a state I don't know, but if they ever come back trying to stake some sort of a claim then I'll just tell them, look, if it wasn't for me this would just be a heap of crumbling wood, all salt-eaten and flaking away. And that's true.

It was a major job making this place liveable, and like

I said before, I had help. I was just desperate for any work when I got into town, and what a stroke of luck, there was this whole bunch of places being built, a big new development.

I guess nice little towns like this appeal to plenty of people who have a bit of money to spend, near the seaside and everything. I'll bet they're getting rarer and rarer too nowadays, these sorts of places.

So what do I do: just walk onto a building site and announce that I want a job. Guys laugh at me, especially being pretty much a kid still, but one of them says if I'm not joking go and speak to somebody in the little plastic office.

They weren't happy about me just strolling in off the street but when I said how desperate I was and how hard I'd work they did say how there are always shirkers in construction, and if I really mean it that I'm going to work hard then they could use me.

The first week was the hardest, mostly because I was having to hassle people to get money for food. I was determined to work like a dog and prove I was worth my while, but when you haven't eaten and the hunger is making you feel like you could pass out on your feet I'm sure you can understand how much harder it gets. Seriously. Plus, naturally on a site you've got a pecking order, and the newer you are and the less useful stuff you know how to do, the harder the work you get.

It was better as I got to know the guys, telling them some of my sob stories about Mum leaving and having to leave home to get away from being with my dad. They softened a bit then, some of them at least, and I'd find people helping me out.

An extra flask of porridge when they came in the morning, maybe a spare sandwich or two or whatever during the day. What a difference. They were a decent bunch once they knew you were going to pull your weight. Once they knew you weren't just some guy going to panhandle them and disappear in a day or two.

All this time I was sleeping rough too. I didn't know anybody nearby, and I didn't want to tell anyone at work how bad it really was. I'd thought to grab a sleeping bag and a few bits and pieces before I left, and for a while I rented hotel rooms – just every few nights as I could barely afford it – not for the bed but to be able to wash.

I didn't have to work too long, though, before I could afford to start renting as a lodger in one of the places I'd seen advertised in town, even if Mrs Kingston, the landlady whose husband had died and who needed the extra money, didn't seem too impressed by the fact I was working on the site. She was just worried about new people moving in and the whole neighbourhood going downhill. I told her I felt the same way, and nothing's worse than people intruding on your own happiness like they've got a right, but still. We can't live in the past.

I can't tell you how it felt, knowing that I was out there, in the world, and paying my own way. But still I missed Natalie. I mean, I missed her all the time. It just felt wrong, like a piece of me was missing, and I couldn't get away from it, that feeling. I went back to see her whenever I could. I had to sneak into the house to avoid Dad. Eventually he changed the locks and then I had to go to the window, trying to get Natalie's attention without him knowing, or when he was out. Yeah, I know, real cute. Like Romeo and Juliet or something.

I missed her more than I can say but there was no way I could go back there, no way in the world with what I had now. I tried to persuade Nat to come with me but she'd always say she had to finish school. I had no time for that. I got jealous, asking if she was talking to anybody there, any boys, but she said no.

She was right in a way and I kind of knew it, but still I had to push it. So she knew how much I missed her. I couldn't invite her there to live out of a backpack with no place to go, or to the room with Mrs Kingston. She'd probably have wanted to know whether we were married or why we were in one bed. She seemed traditional like that.

That was probably part or even most of why I had the whole idea, walking on the beach, seeing it. The old beach house. It was a vision, really, to even see it as somewhere to live, the way it looked.

It was small, but what did that matter? Just a couple of rooms up some steps propped up on logs, half spilling out straight onto the beach. Bits were rotten but we looked into it, guys from the site who knew more than I did, even though I'd been picking the trade up quickly, and doing my best to.

Bits were rotten but not any of the most important bits. The wood had been treated or something, so it wasn't as bad as it looked like it could be, if you were determined, which I was, and had a little help available, which I managed to get.

So I had a vision and a mission and I was working overtime for the money, and I saved and told people who I trusted and who needed to know, managing to rope them in for money sometimes but mostly favours and friendship. You know, I think that people kind of like me sometimes. I don't know why; maybe because I'm mostly honest and don't have a problem with anybody unless they have a problem with me. Even if I can be kind of blunt sometimes, people like that.

So I roped people in and it gradually shaped up and I couldn't believe it that here it was happening, and when it was finished we had a little party there on the beach. I had to do that for everybody, to celebrate and show my gratitude, and they knew what it meant to me given I'd told them about how I'd ended up where I am. I told them – more or less, anyway. Sometimes you have to be careful, with anybody, no matter how friendly.

If I told you how I felt just being able to rent a room, imagine how this was for me. The icing on the cake of escape. More than that. This was my own place, by the sea, a beach house, half found, half built myself. And what a place. What a dream! It was like everything was finally getting to be how it should be. Almost like I could find faith in miracles, and of course then I knew I'd be able to get Natalie out here and away from our dad. Not stuck in that hellhole with him. That was all I could think about really, and it didn't matter how long it took to make it happen because time didn't matter, it just had to be that way. It had to be.

That was what was going to happen, and when it was done I still had to twist her arm – she still wanted to finish school – but I knew that she was just like me really, and more than anything, more than school, she wanted us both to be together. We were twins and it was special. We had to be together, and so eventually she agreed. At first just to come out and see it, and stay for one night maybe. But that was it. She wasn't going back, not ever. This was her home now. Here with me.

She would say she felt bad about leaving Dad like that, but I couldn't find it in myself to feel guilt or shame. We weren't going to let him know anything, not where we were or how to reach us, nothing like that. I was just too happy to feel bad. We'd made it. We'd escaped. I told her that all of that was in the past and not anything worth thinking of or worrying about. We were together and that was the future for us now.

Maybe it's sexist but I thought it worked fine with me out at work and Nat at home. She could look after the place and we'd work on the beach and collect shells and pretty stones and anything else she could make into jewellery.

Natalie would go into town shopping and getting to know the locals. I thought they were a bit busybody and gossipy to be honest, but it was great if it was making her happy. That was all I wanted.

There were little town events and sometimes touristy things and she was able to sell her jewellery and other things she did, like her cooking. She loved all of that; she got really good. I still had friends on the site but I tended not to bother with them out of work, even if some of them dropped hints angling to come over, try some of Nat's cooking or whatever.

One thing is that we never told anybody who we really were. I mean, they knew our first names and we invented second names and we told people that we were living together – that's not a lie – but did not say brother and sister. Even when they said things about how we could be, given how similar we looked. We'd always been like that; people just took us to be a couple and we let them. I told Nat that we should. Apart from anything else, there was our dad still out there somewhere to think about. Who knows how people find things out?

So we were happy to my mind, and if this story could end there, well, wouldn't that be a nice story with a happy ending. But it doesn't. It doesn't end there, because – who knew what would happen? Out of everything that could possibly happen – well, what do you think?

He came back.

He found us. That's right. 'Him', our father, of all people, came to pay us a visit. Just sauntered up the beach one day to see Natalie sitting out on our stairs as I imagine it, maybe distracted reading a book or making some jewellery, the way that she could fill her days however she wanted, distracted until he was right up next to her and said her name. I don't know, I wasn't there. I was out at work.

I was out at work and what a thing to come back to, happily calling out to Nat as I got close, wondering what the evening was going to be, and she came out with a bit of a serious look and I could tell something was up before I got up the stairs to see him sitting in our house, in the beach house, the place that I'd pretty much built myself.

There was nothing there for him and no reason for him to be there. He tried to smile at me, kind of weakly, and I didn't do anything in response. What was I going to say to him? Nat tried to smooth things over of course; she said why don't we two go for a walk on the beach together while she made food. I could've just left then, but I guess that would've been a tantrum. Why should I leave my own home when somebody you can't stand having there rolls in?

I said something about how many people she was cooking for but she was insistent we should talk, me and our dad, it was important and please, and that's how I ended up with him, walking along the beach, side by side, and it was awkward.

Awkward as he tried to open up about so many things that it was all too late to discuss, when I was determined to have nothing between us, and I felt I was making it pretty clear.

He had some rambling stories. Told me wow, I've really built a life for myself out here, like he was proud, as though he had any stake in me and my life.

He said it made him think of how it was at first with him and Mum, starting off in a shotgun shack without even a spare room, working every hour he could to pay for raising two kids. They'd only really been planning on one and he was kind of worried about that, but Mum was determined.

Said he couldn't do that work now he was older. Said what it is to be younger, trying to make a joke of it; said I must know plenty of that kind of back-breaking labour now. Nat had been telling him things.

Tried to ask me if I could remember that place. Us two must've been three or four when they left; he was made site supervisor so they could get a place with a room for me and Nat, a separate kitchen, a few things like the television and whatever else.

I didn't want to hear any of this. Then it got into the moaning, the self-pity. I couldn't stand it, like he was trying to blackmail me. Where could he go from there? He had no qualifications and he was getting older, and still having to work. Not being a people person, what could he do in an office?

I guess he must've been frustrated I was giving no ground. All I could think about was getting him away from here. I didn't care. I just wanted him gone. Did I realise now how hard he was working to get these things, to keep our family together and moving forward?

I remember some stuff pretty clearly. It got intense. He stopped to look at me, having walked a fair way from the house, the light beginning to dwindle as the sun slipped into the water of the horizon.

'Look, Nicky. I know I can't say I was a perfect dad, but I can't unlive my life. Will you talk to me? We're all adults now. Do you think I worked for fun? Who was putting bread on the table? You think I made no sacrifices?'

'Well, like you say, we're all adults now. If you're miserable you've only got yourself to blame, and it's your own problem so I don't know why you're here.'

'Yeah, why I'm here...' He looked away then back to me. I just stared at him.

'And that's it then, is it?' he said.

Another long hard cold pause.

'After all I've done you're just gonna...'

'Yeah, after everything you've done. Exactly.' It hurt to have him here, like he was stepping on me, and I was sick of it; I could feel it like bile rising up from the back of my throat. Why was he here now? What did he want? What had he turned up expecting from me? From us?

He moved close. I could smell his breath and I shoved him back. He scowled and hissed in frustration. Something in me was just about ready to snap and when he moved closer again I couldn't tell if it was to try and hug me or what but I'd just had enough; I swung at him and he was ready for it too; he slammed me right around the head and I went down.

Part of me wasn't expecting this. A voice in my head was saying it was foolish, ugly and wrong, but it was only one small, shrill little voice and it didn't have control of me.

It was just the pure luck of feeling a good solid fist-sized rock near my hand as I sprawled in the sand, reaching out after he'd hit me, and when he came over he seemed apologetic as much as aggressive.

I don't know if I really expected him to just fall down with one good firm swing from the rock like that. There was a dull whoompf and a slightly wet sort of cracking sound as it thudded into his temple, leaving him reeling a little, holding his head and moaning. Not screaming at the top of his voice but this dull moaning, like slaughtered cattle it seemed to me somehow, dull and dumb and senseless and just worth slaughtering and nothing more.

I remember looking at the blood from his head spilling out onto the soft yellow sand as he went down. There was still enough light to see where it touched the sand and got eaten up into grains. It didn't look like blood anymore, it was just wet sand. It could be anything really.

It was impulse that made me lash out the first time, but it was something different that made me carry on. Some feeling of having everything I loved and everything I was, my whole being – whether it had come from effort or luck or somebody else's kindness – all of it soiled completely, forever. That made me carry on.

I carried on smashing this moaning old man's head with the rock still in my hand, beating his skull in. 'Nicky,' he was mumbling, I think. 'Nicky.' He put his hands up and I had to kick them away but I kept bashing until he stopped making noise and wasn't moving.

He looked dead but I wanted to be sure, so I dragged him down to the water and into it, enough to cover him completely. He still didn't move. Face down in the damp sand with water splashing up over his whole body. That was good. I threw the rock as far out as I could into the sea. I went back, kicking over all the sand where I'd dragged him and over any blood, right up to where we'd fought, to conceal every trace of the drama from minutes before.

I checked every few seconds behind me to see if he was moving in the water. He wasn't. He was dead. For certain.

My heart was pounding in my head like I can't say, but nobody was there, nobody could've seen anything. I couldn't see anyone anyway.

I ran back to Natalie and told her. It was an accident; we'd fought but I never meant to kill him. I was upset and I threw a rock at him before storming off to calm down, I said; he must've been concussed and stumbled into the sea and drowned.

Natalie trusted me, as awful as it was, and we knew that we had to do something. There was a tourist place less than an hour's walk away where you could hire out boats. We decided to keep his body hidden for now and when we got back here with the boat, we'd take his body out as far as we could go, tie it down with rocks and throw it overboard. Nobody would find it. Nobody would know it was there. Take fishing stuff just in case anybody saw us and wondered why we were out there. Even if they saw over the edge, he could just be sleeping.

I did it alone and what a way – the last time I saw my father – can you imagine it? I heaved him over the edge to sink down into the ocean and be gone forever. I remember his cheap trousers and tacky shirt. I decided to strip him naked and then burn everything separately. It seemed safer, a more anonymous body. Less to identify him.

I cut everything into little strips and burned them all up – wallet, cards; I kept the keys – melted everything plastic into black lumps of stinking nothingness, then threw them away, each into separate bins all around town. Just to be sure.

That was fear, pure fear, and it was exhilaration which I have nothing else in my life to compare to. I guess I can see how murder can become an addiction. I heard once about how the most successful serial killer of all time would just drive halfway across the country at the weekends to some random new city and kill a new victim somewhere like a dark alley and drive home miles away and nobody could catch him because how could you possibly trace it back and find him?

I think he handed himself in eventually.

He was crazy, though, always killing young women and talking about their 'evil eyes', and I wasn't crazy and

I'm not even sure there was anybody else I wanted dead, I just didn't see why I should be punished for what I did.

I think that I prayed to a god I didn't believe in. Maybe I prayed for forgiveness, I don't remember, but I know I must have prayed just to be left alone and not be punished for my crime. I just wanted to get away with it.

I prayed my fake little prayer, feigning belief, and wondered if it was the same for everybody who prays, desperately feigning belief because they've got some deep dark secret as a reason to make them pretend.

Maybe not.

Maybe I'm an evil person and I'm going to hell. Maybe there's something bad and wrong inside me and I deserve it. I don't know. I'm just somebody trying to live my life, you know?

Nothing happened anyway. Nothing happened, nobody got suspicious, nobody came to ask questions. There was no investigation as far as I know.

It made me think what a sad, lonely nobody my father was. Maybe that made me feel better. Kind of as though it was a mercy killing. I must've put him out of his misery. That's how I think about it sometimes. No funeral for him, nobody cared. Nobody missed him then and nobody misses him now either.

The house that we grew up in was empty now. Our house. The idea came, that I could go back... but I thought better of it. I could've taken the car. No way.

But you need to know what I found out, not long after. Why he was there in the first place.

Natalie told me what he'd never managed to. Our mum had died. Her family had been in touch with him because they thought he should know. Her funeral was happening. She'd killed herself.

Natalie was scared. I was scared. I was numb with fear. At first anyway. It was all I could think about. I couldn't sleep. I got the shakes. At work they told me I didn't look well and that I should take time off. I couldn't; it made me feel worse having nothing to do. I needed to take my mind off things. I wanted normality again.

One thing that never worried me was Natalie. I knew that even with this, she wouldn't betray me. How could she? We were twins. We loved each other. As far back as I could remember we'd always been together. Always. And somehow I felt that as long as we were together it would be okay. I would always be there for her and do anything for her. It would be okay. As long as I had her.

As for Mum's funeral, we both felt weird about the whole thing. At first it was me saying I felt like we could keep all of that in the past and put it behind us and get on with our own lives. Even though we loved her. We had our own life now... but Nat was saying no, we had to go, how could we not? She was our mother! Then we'd both kind of change our minds mutually and use each other to help think about everything. Anyway, we made it in the end, and I'm glad we did.

We managed to borrow smart things to wear from people we knew that pretty much fit. All funerals must be strange, but maybe this one especially. Definitely, all things considered.

If I looked shaken then people must've put it down to grief, I think. Grief for my mum, I mean. She had so much family. I never realised. I think Dad must've cut them out, like the miserable loner he was. I couldn't stand his self-pity. She had five brothers and sisters and all of them had children, I think; there must've been about a dozen of them, all different ages. It was hard to take in. They were all sad and sorry and friendly.

One of her brothers couldn't hold back his tears. I'd never seen that before, a grown man crying. He was shaking while he sobbed.

Natalie was better at talking to people. She was always good at that. I never know what to say. I think she was really taken by the whole thing. I think the guy crying was the last person to see Mum alive. Mum had stayed with all different people since leaving.

I remember feeling mostly numb at the funeral. Maybe shocked. I try to remember whether I was sad, and I'm sure that I was. It wasn't that she was dead – it was that she'd failed. She never managed to escape.

I was used to Mum being gone, that had happened ages ago. I'd accepted it and got on with my own things. I'd been busy and I guess I just thought, or hoped, that she'd gone off and done her own thing too. That she'd escaped Dad and managed to find happiness. But she hadn't. She'd just messed up and failed and killed herself.

I guess that maybe Dad had a point when he'd call Mum crazy. I mean, he could be right. You have to be crazy to kill yourself, don't you? I don't know.

You know, sometimes I wonder how Dad found us. Natalie says he just came on something of a hunch. He was going to come anyway, hearing about the death, to this place where we all used to holiday, like in the picture. Maybe he did.

Had Mum ever tried to find us? I don't know. She'd only have had Dad to contact. Neither of us told anybody about this place. It was a new start out here. Natalie wouldn't have told anybody. And how could mum have stood going back there to him?

Natalie wanted to go to the wake after the formal ceremony. I probably wouldn't have otherwise. It was all people I didn't know. They pretty much all seemed to have known Mum when she was young, it seemed. Like when she got with Dad and had us her life kind of ended. I guess she was bringing us up. That's something serious, raising kids.

People gave Natalie their numbers but we didn't have a phone at the beach house. We didn't even have an address to send post to. Some of them gave us their addresses and said we'd have to get in touch. It was a nice gesture, certainly, but I didn't really take any of it seriously.

I think Natalie was taken by the whole thing though. Family. It wasn't long after that – I think she'd really warmed to the idea – she wanted a child of her own. She wouldn't stop talking about it. What was I supposed to do? She was my twin and I loved her and I only wanted to make her happy. That meant everything in the world to me. It always had done and now more than ever.

What was I supposed to do?

Sometimes parents say you don't know how it feels to become one until it happens. That you simply can't understand.

I look at other parents and I'm still not sure they quite feel exactly how I do about Amy, and have done right from the first moment I saw her.

It was like the start of something but also it felt like the end of something too. This was like freedom, and a new life. I felt born again, with everything from the past washed away and cleansed, and in a way that's what I'd always been crying out for.

Seeing Amy there so tiny and soft and pure and innocent I just wanted to protect her and keep her safe and make everything in the world pure and perfect and special forever and ever for our little Amy, Amy whose name begins with an 'A' like the start of the alphabet.

Just this soft tiny little thing lying there smiling and reaching out, this soft tiny little thing, a vulnerable little being Natalie had made for us, suddenly there in a world full of danger and harshness and everything broken and twisted and wrong. Still, amongst all that, there she was.

And you know, for a while, it was perfect. Everything was just perfect. I mean, I couldn't believe it. I couldn't have been happier. Literally nothing in the world could've been better than the three of us together. If there was a heaven, I didn't care. This beat it.

Happiness can be one of the strangest things to feel alone. You want to share it with the whole world and have everybody feel this satisfied and complete, but somehow I was also glad to keep the world at arm's length and have it going on in the background, no matter how overjoyed I was with happiness spilling over.

Maybe that's my problem. Because this is where it all comes out now. I'm trying to be honest with you, as honest as I can be. It got difficult.

I never thought it would, but it did. After all we'd been through I didn't see it coming and I still can't believe it. How could it happen? I already admitted I'm not perfect.

I guess she wasn't happy. How could that be? Not happy with the thought of being here forever, me on a builder's wage, struggling to make ends meet you could say, now with Amy to look after. But what does that matter if you're happy? And I thought we were. I was so happy.

She wanted Amy to do better than us. You know, an education. A proper one, college or whatever, and – well, maybe I didn't take to that too well.

I mean, there I was – didn't she realise just how hard I was working? I was doing everything for this house and for our family. Doing everything I could to keep us all together and happy. How could she say that she wasn't happy? We had everything. We were free!

But I guess – I mean, I can see why she might have

felt trapped, because I did too, in a way. And I guess my prospects ultimately were kind of limited. Both of us were kind of limited like that. And so yes, Amy too.

I can see that now, and I can see how maybe I wasn't so clear-headed when we were talking about it, and how it came to arguing and how no, that's not a happy family anymore. And maybe arguing about nothing sometimes. Or about something I didn't know.

But there were times – I couldn't believe it – she would say she was scared for Amy. Scared! As if I would ever... as if I could even think about that. Anything like that. As if I have it in me.

But well – what does it matter now anyway, you know? She's gone.

My sister. My twin sister. Natalie's gone. Natalie who was always there for me and who I always loved, and always put first.

She's gone. She ran away and she took Amy with her too. They escaped, I guess. They escaped. And from what? From me.

So I'm here alone now, and what can I do? I've still got the house. I don't know what I can do, or where I can go. And hey, who knows, if I stay maybe she'll just turn up some day, you know? Maybe she'll come back.

Well, it's not going to happen if I leave. Or maybe one day the police will be here asking questions. I mean, they haven't yet, so she hasn't done anything like that, and that counts for something, doesn't it?

So that's it really, my whole story spelled out for

you, and I wonder what you might make of it now I've confessed, if that's what this is. You know, I don't sleep so well anymore. Maybe I need a doctor. I think about my dad and I have these nightmares of his rotting body climbing up the shore. I wake up in the night and think he's come back. I have dreams where I'm turning over every stone on the beach. The bed burns for me now and I feel a loneliness like never before. Everybody's gone and I keep on going, but in a way... in a way all I can feel is jealousy for the people around me, all of who have managed to escape, while I'm left here. And I think about this house I built, pretty much anyway, and how it was a happy home for a while and I think about how it would be if I was gone, and how long it would take to crumble down to the bare timbers, wood and rotting fabric eaten by the salt spray from the sea, collapsing softly inwards upon itself.

WINONA THE ANGELIC WIZARD

RICHARD BASKETT

Winona was a helpful young woman with short blonde pixie hair, a college graduate and a loving granddaughter. She lived in a small neighbourhood just outside the Lake District with her border collie, Cody.

One day, Winona and Cody were at the office of her grandma's lawyer, Charlotte Zellinski. She was an old hag of an attorney, about seventy-six years old, and she smoked using a very small cigarette holder.

'Now then, my dear,' said Charlotte, as she put on her reading glasses and picked up a piece of paper. It was Winona's grandma's will. 'First of all, I'm deeply sorry for the terrible passing of your beloved grandma.'

Winona and Cody lowered their heads in sadness and tried not to cry.

'Right then, let's see what your grandma has to say in her will.'

Winona and Cody leaned forward to listen as Charlotte read the document.

'I, Georgette Wizzin, wish to leave everything I own to my loving granddaughter, Winona Wizzin. She is my loyal and only benefactor, since the rest of my family moved away to Italy and never came back.'

Winona was amazed. 'Oh my gosh! I'm her only benefactor? What did she leave me?'

'Well,' replied Charlotte, 'she has left three things that she wishes to hand over to you.'

'What are they?' asked Winona.

Charlotte took another look at the will. 'The first thing is her luxury bungalow in the middle of the forest just outside Edinburgh. The second thing is that she wants you to take great care of her group of talking animals who live in the bungalow, and the last thing is...'

'What is it?'

'Well, did your grandma ever tell you she used to be a wizard?' asked Charlotte.

Yes, she had. Winona cast her mind back to when she was six or seven, when she had first discovered that her grandma was a wizard. Winona remembered her grandma showing her a few magic spells and tricks, like making kitchen equipment fly around the ceiling and how to make magic potions with odd ingredients. Winona had been so amazed, and vowed to keep her grandma's secret safe.

Winona's childhood flashbacks faded from her mind and she looked at Charlotte. 'Yes, of course. Her magic was so amazing that I sometimes wished I could be like her.'

'Well, now you can, my dear! The last thing your grandma left you is actually a request – she wants you to take her place and carry on her wizardry legacy.'

Charlotte gave the will to Winona. 'Wow. Thank you, Grandma,' Winona whispered.

Charlotte pulled out a large, ancient book and a long, thin brass wand from under her desk and placed them in front of Winona. 'Here, your grandma's book of magic spells and her solid brass wand,' she said, taking a puff from her cigarette holder.

'Oh, I remember those,' smiled Winona. She picked up the wand, opened the book and started turning the pages. She found the page she was looking for. 'Bingo! The animal speaking spell.'

Winona looked down at Cody. 'Hold still, Cody. I'm going to try this spell on you.' Cody walked backwards a little bit and whimpered. 'Right, here goes. Diseasel schizeasel!' Winona waved the magic wand and pointed it at Cody. A speck of magic dust flew straight down his throat. He coughed loudly and started to speak. 'Oh, yuck! That stuff tastes like a bunch of dead flies!'

Winona and Charlotte laughed and shook hands.

The next day, Winona and Cody moved out of their neighbourhood and began driving north towards the forest near Edinburgh to go and live at Winona's grandma's bungalow.

'Winona, I want some clothes!' groaned Cody. 'I feel cold and nude.'

'Stop that complaining, Cody. We're almost there, so be patient.'

In no time at all, Winona and Cody had arrived at the luxury bungalow in the middle of the forest. It was beautiful; all the walls were painted dark blue with little white stars, and the front garden had an enormous oak tree with a door-sized hollow at the bottom.

'Here it is, Cody,' said Winona, sighing. 'Grandma's wizard bungalow. Our new home.'

She stopped the car in front of the house, got out with Cody and walked towards the silver-painted front door. *I can't wait to meet Grandma's talking animals*, she thought. *I wonder if they're magical as well.*

Before Winona could open the front door, she and Cody heard screams coming from inside the house. 'HELP! HELP!'

'Hey, someone's in trouble!' shouted Cody.

'You're right, and it came from the front window.'

Winona and Cody ran up to the front window and looked through. Hundreds of kitchen items – pots, pans, plates, cutlery – were flying everywhere, and millions of soapy bubbles were pouring out of the kitchen sink and floating around the entire house.

'Gadzooks!' shouted Winona.

'Holy hawk toes!' gulped Cody.

Winona and Cody saw two animals in a terrible state of panic. One was a dark green iguana, who looked highly strung and was pacing up and down the kitchen like mad, and the other was a black queen cat with a pencil resting on top of her left ear, peeking out from under a red silky pillow.

'Somebody help us!' screamed the iguana.

'We can't control all this magical chaos!' cried the cat.

'Don't worry, I'm coming!' Winona took out the

magic wand from her pocket and ran through the front door. She tried to remember the magic word to stop all spells. She thought harder back to her childhood. At last she remembered. She waved the magic wand. 'Ali kazap!'

With a great crash and clatter, all the bubbles disappeared into thin air and all the kitchen equipment fell to the floor. The cat and the iguana came out from hiding. They looked relieved to see that the magical chaos had stopped.

'What just happened?' asked the iguana.

'I have no idea,' said the cat.

Winona cleared her throat. The two animals turned their heads to see her and Cody standing in front of the open doorway.

The iguana grinned. 'Georgette? Is that you?'

'No, it isn't,' fumed the cat. 'She's far too young to be Georgette.'

'That's her granddaughter, Winona,' said a voice. It sounded old. Winona looked to her right. A large green fish with a goatee beard popped out of an aquarium tank. 'Hey there, my love. I'm Grandpa Kipper and it's so delightful to see you at last.'

Winona walked towards Grandpa Kipper's tank, confused. 'Why did Grandma call you Grandpa Kipper? You're not related to her, are you?'

'Oh, heavens no,' he chuckled. 'She just called me that because I talk like an old sea dog codger.'

'A sea dog?' asked Cody. 'Dogs can live under the sea?'

Grandpa Kipper chortled and shook his head. 'No, my furry lad. A sea dog is a sailor who travelled the seven seas in the good old days. Why, I remember my first trip, swimming the Atlantic Ocean—'

'Thank you, Grandpa Kipper, that'll do,' interrupted the iguana. Grandpa Kipper sighed and sank back down into his tank.

'So, who are you guys?' asked Winona, turning to the iguana and the cat.

'My name's Hayley,' said the cat. 'I'm your grandma's wizard secretary.'

'My name's Brandon,' said the iguana. 'And I serve as the caretaker to this bungalow.'

Winona shook Brandon's claw and Hayley's paw. 'Nice to meet you. So, tell me, what happened with all the kitchen stuff and the bubbles flying everywhere?'

They both looked puzzled. 'Who knows?' said Hayley. 'We were busy having breakfast. Then a small voice whispered a magic spell and made everything in the kitchen come to life.'

'Yeah. And I want to know who whispered that spell,' muttered Brandon, gravely.

'Shush!' said Winona. 'I can hear voices.' They listened carefully, and could hear the faint sounds of whispering and rustling coming from behind the blue door of the food cupboard.

Cody sniffed. 'Never mind the voices. I can smell a dirty something.'

Winona had an idea. 'Cody! Go into the food cupboard and have a sniff. But don't eat the food!'

Cody groaned and pushed the kitchen stepladder up to the cupboard and opened the cupboard door with his paws. He started to climb up the ladder to sniff the shelves. He ignored a six-pack of clear lemonade bottles, a ready-to-be-eaten meat pie and a plate of homemade lemon curd tarts. At last, he reached the top shelf and looked around. Suddenly, he saw a small sack move sideways.

'Hmm.' He picked up the sack in his mouth and shook it. Voices came from inside.

'Hey, stop it!'

'Yeah, I'm going to be sick from all that shaking!'

'Shut up, you two! We've been ratted out!'

Cody tipped the sack upside down and out came three mischievous rats. They fell straight into a beef and pork aspic on the bottom shelf. Cody laughed as he climbed down.

'Winona!' he shouted. 'I found the voices and I've trapped them inside this aspic.'

'Well done, Cody. Bring them out of the cupboard and we'll see who those voices belong to.'

The cupboard door opened and out came Cody pushing the aspic on a plate with the three rats trapped inside.

'Well, well, well. Monty, Raquel and Irwin,' said Hayley.

'So, you three whispered that magic spell, just so you could help yourselves to all the food in the cupboard?' said Brandon, rolling up a newspaper.

'Yeah. I want a chocolate biscuit!' said Irwin, a stupid dark brown rat in a green and yellow stripy nightcap.

'Shut up, Irwin! I'm sick of you always whining for biscuits,' grumbled Raquel, a hot-headed light tan rat wearing a small gold necklace.

'Will you two be quiet? We're in big trouble right now!' whispered Monty, a smart light brown rat with a tiny French moustache.

The three rats cowered in the aspic when they saw Hayley and Brandon leaning down towards them with cross looks on their faces and rolled-up newspapers in their claws.

'Calm down, guys!' begged Winona. 'Violence doesn't solve anything. We'll just do a little interrogation of these three rats.'

The three rats had soon been pulled out of the aspic and were sitting on the kitchen table, all tied up together with bits of string.

'What are they going to do to us, boss?' asked Irwin.

'I don't know, but don't worry, just let me do the talking,' said Monty.

Winona, Cody, Hayley and Brandon gathered around the rats, ready to ask them a series of questions.

'Now then. Tell us the truth,' said Brandon, pompously. 'Did you three whisper that "come alive" magic spell behind our backs?'

'No, we didn't,' said Monty.

'I think someone is telling porky pies,' hissed Hayley.

'We're not!' said Raquel.

Hayley, Brandon and the three rats went on and on arguing, until Cody got so fed up he gave a loud howl of rage. 'Silence! This isn't a pantomime!'

Cody took deep breaths to calm himself and Winona stroked his head.

'Calm down, Cody. Look, I think I have an idea to crack those rats.'

The rats looked at each other, worried, wondering what Winona was going to do to them.

'Guys, bring in Grandpa Kipper,' ordered Winona, a wicked grin on her face.

The three rats turned pale when they heard the name.

'No, no, not Grandpa Kipper!' said Monty.

'We can't stand his stories about his youth in the deep blue sea!' said Raquel.

'They're SO boring!' said Irwin.

But Winona and the animals didn't listen. They'd already put earmuffs over their ears when they put Grandpa Kipper in a large fishbowl and placed him on the kitchen table.

Grandpa Kipper began. 'When I was living in the ocean, me and my friend Scowley the seahorse came across a whole army of sharks swimming across the Pacific. They were planning to attack a colony of octopuses. But Scowley and I had a plan.'

The rats tossed and turned. Grandpa Kipper had only just begun but the rats could stand no more.

'Alright, alright! It was us!' shouted Monty. 'We whispered that magic spell.'

'Happy now?' shrieked Raquel. 'Now please, make Grandpa Kipper stop!'

Winona and the animals smiled. They had finally made the rats tell the truth. They took Grandpa Kipper off the table and put him back into his aquarium.

'Thanks for your help, Grandpa Kipper,' said Winona.

'Think nothing of it,' he smiled. 'Glad to help, anytime.'

As he swam back down into his tank, Winona walked over to the table to untie the three rats.

'You three should be ashamed of yourselves! Never play around with magic. It's not a toy.'

The three rats bowed their heads.

'We're sorry,' murmured Monty.

'You're not going to throw us out of the house, are you?' asked Irwin, looking worried.

'Well, since you three are my grandma's talking animals, I won't do that. I'm just going to send you back into your chest of drawers. Hayley told me where you came from.'

Winona picked up her wand, waved it and said the magic word. 'Abracapocus.'

Quick as a flash, the three rats were back in their chest of drawers. Winona took a bow and Cody, Hayley and Brandon gave her a big round of applause.

'Thank you, thank you!' smiled Winona, walking towards the front door.

'Wait! Where are you going?' asked Brandon.

'You're leaving?' said Hayley.

Winona turned round. 'Well, I...' She stopped. Hayley and Brandon looked sad. 'What's the matter, guys?' she asked.

'Oh, nothing. It's just that things haven't been easy in this house ever since Georgette disappeared,' sighed Hayley.

'She was so ill. The ambulance took her to the hospital and she never came back,' said Brandon, tears starting to fall from his eyes. He put his face in his hands. Winona felt sorry for him. She walked to the table and picked him up to hug him.

'Sweetie, I'm not leaving,' she said. 'I'm just going to get my luggage from the car and bring it inside.'

Brandon stopped crying and looked up at Winona's face in surprise. 'You're moving in?'

Winona nodded with a smile.

'You're staying?' asked Hayley, looking happy.

'Of course, I am. You see, my grandma wrote a will before she disappeared. She left me everything that belonged to her – the bungalow, and you guys – and she wanted me to carry on her wizardry legacy.'

Hayley and Brandon were happy to hear the wonderful news.

'Oh, thank you, Winona,' said Brandon, as she put him back down on the table.

A few minutes later, Winona finished unpacking her luggage with her magic wand. She looked up to see a large painted portrait of her grandma hanging over the mantelpiece. She was smiling, the magic wand in her hand.

'Don't worry, Grandma,' said Winona. 'Your legacy as a wizard will continue.'

She heard a throat clearing behind her, and turned to see Hayley and Brandon holding out a huge indigo robe to her.

'My grandma's wizard robe!' gasped Winona.

'Well, since you're taking over from Georgette, you'd better wear it,' said Brandon.

Winona put on her grandma's robe. It fitted her perfectly. Hayley showed her what she looked like in a mirror.

'Wow, I look amazing! What do you think, Cody?'

'Not as glamorous as me,' said Cody, as he appeared wearing a royal guard's uniform. 'Finally, some clothes for me to wear.'

'You deserve it, Cody,' grinned Hayley, as she held the mirror up for him. 'It was you who caught those trouble-making rats and stopped their mischief-making.'

A while later Charlotte came to the bungalow to see how Winona was getting on. Winona told her there had been a few magical problems, but everything had come right in the end.

Winona, Charlotte and the animals sat down around the table with glasses of clear lemonade. They raised them up high to toast Winona for saving the bungalow, and to welcome her as the new wizard.

'Three cheers for Winona!' said Hayley, proudly.

Charlotte and the animals shouted 'Hip hip hooray!' three times, and Winona shed a happy tear.

And so that was Winona's story, of how she took her grandma's place as a wizard, and had magical adventures with her talking animal friends.

ACKNOWLEDGEMENTS

Jon Adams

'A Conversation of Sparrows' is my first published short story and I am indebted to Mainspring Arts and the other participants for enabling me to set a part of my PTSD and internal narrative free. I have lived most of my life in the dark, only discovering later in life an explanation for my differences that have made life hard at times, but also explaining the unique autistic experience of the world and that my creativity has value.

Richard Baskett

Richard would like to thank his uncle Steven for taking him to London to take part in the Square Peg Stories course, and his uncle Anthony for making it possible for him to attend the Orpheus Centre.

Esther Lowery

Esther would like to thank her family and friends for their help and support, especially her mother who took her down to London for the Square Peg Stories course. Her dog wasn't actually born when she initially wrote her short story, but he was great support once he came into existence. She would also like to thank the guest authors from the Square Peg team for all of their help.

Luke Matthews

I want to offer my huge thanks to my family and everybody involved in the Square Peg Stories scheme, and also the staff from Specialist Autism Services; without all of these people, their goodwill and their generosity, I don't see how I could possibly have been able to achieve what I have.

Kate Roy

Thanks to my family, friends and teachers who are too numerous to name; to my fellow *In Other Words* contributors; and to Baby Yoda for teaching us all how to love again. And to you for picking up this book.

Sarah

Sarah would like to thank her husband, family and friends, and all her pets, for their love and support.

Damian Sawyer

Damian sends heartfelt thanks to his family and friends for their support and encouragement, especially to Ian Cutler for encouraging him to contribute. He sends congratulations to his fellow writers! He thanks the Square Peg Stories mentors, Unbound and all who pre-ordered, for dreaming, encouraging creativity and cultivating this anthology. To his fiancée, Carol, he says, 'Here's to the stories that brought us together and all the ones we have yet to write!'

Wiskey
For Honder and for Pomme with great gratitude.

From all the contributors
The contributors would like to thank Katya and Miranda at Mainspring Arts for running the Square Peg Stories scheme, and for their support.

Mainspring Arts
Mainspring Arts would like to thank the Square Peg Stories tutors and mentors: Joanne Limburg, Jonathan Totman, Adam Feinstein, Corinne Duyvis, Emma Claire Sweeney, Giancarlo Gemin and Eliza Robertson. Thank you also to David Mitchell and Jill Dawson for their advice, time and enthusiasm. Thanks to the wonderful volunteers who helped with the running of the project, and Riverside Studios, who kindly donated their space for us to use. Thank you to DeAndra, Fiona and the rest of the team at Unbound for bringing our book to life. Finally, this book would not have been possible without the generous support of the AOK Trust and Arts Council England. Thank you all for raising and amplifying neurodivergent voices.

THE CONTRIBUTORS

Jon Adams

Jon is a polymath artist working cross-platform in image, poetry, sound, performance and spoken word, referencing synaesthesia, autism, dyslexia, autobiography, science and hidden metaphor. This results in unique visual perspectives of systemising history, time and place. After training as a palaeontologist he spent thirty years as a book illustrator but recently received social engaged commissions from London 2012, UK Parliament, which have evolved into performance after working with Sir Peter Brook as a synaesthete. He also actively promotes research into autistic mental health and suicide in autism, and advocates for the dismantling of barriers to arts inclusion and for the autistic narrative to rest firmly in autistic people's hands.

Richard Baskett

Born in Croydon in 1991, Richard Baskett loved coming up with stories throughout his childhood. He gets his inspiration for his stories from his experiences growing up. While attending the Orpheus Centre in Godstone to learn how to become a proper writer, he won a contest to take part in the Square Peg Stories writers' course.

Esther Lowery

Esther is an avid writer from Holywell in North Wales, who was diagnosed as autistic in 2015 at the age of seventeen. She currently holds a bachelor's degree in English Literature and Creative Writing from the Open University and is studying for an advanced undergraduate diploma in Local History from Oxford University. Esther has been writing since she was a young child and has written several full novel drafts. In her spare time, she enjoys crime shows, listening to music, reading and playing with her family's cowardly pet dog, Odysseus, as well as avoiding as much human contact as possible.

Luke Matthews

Luke lives in an attic flat above a pub, without pets, family or any of those other irritating distractions, and hopes that one day all of the time he spends writing could at least go some way towards funding the stupendous caffeine consumption apparently associated with this habit. He has recently turned forty, can still remember when his whole life was stretching out ahead of him, and wonders what happened exactly.

Kate Roy

Kate is an aspiring writer with Asperger's syndrome. Born in Dundee in 1991, her life story could not be more clichéd: she struggled to fit in and connect with people growing up so she retreated into her imagination to cope. She created entire universes there and hopes to share them with the world through her writing. She loves walruses and the moon, and doesn't understand how people can function without maladaptive daydreaming. She currently resides in the city where she was born and her hobbies include gardening, hoarding stuffed animals and petting other people's dogs.

Sarah

Sarah was diagnosed on the autistic spectrum at twenty-five years old. She has been writing poems and stories for as long as she can remember, and she is really excited that this is her first published story. Sarah lives with her husband and three cats, and they are expecting their first child, who will have been born by the time you read this.

Damian Sawyer

Damian Sawyer is a poet, writer, digital artist and musician. He was born in 1972 in Portsmouth, England. In 1990 he moved to Cardiff, Wales, to study BSc Astrophysics. His daughter and two sons were born and raised there. He had several poems published in *Paving the Way* (Glenwood Writer's Group, 2006) and his short story 'Death-Dealer' was included in the audio anthology *Doctor Who – Short Trips vol.1* (Big Finish, 2010). His writing has diverse inspirations including social justice, spirituality, physics, etymology, philosophy and ecology. He was diagnosed as having Asperger's syndrome in 2016, at the age of forty-four.

Wiskey

Wiskey describes himself as a 'living artist'. He has dedicated his working life to producing large colourful, powerful paintings, but is also a traditional storyteller, photographer and writer of short stories, poetry and art theory. More recently he's started making documentary films and is deeply concerned with the question: what makes a piece of art sacred? Wiskey was diagnosed as High Functioning Autistic in 2015, at the age of fifty, which has been a major turning point in his creative and day-to-day experience of life. He lives in West London.

Unbound is the world's first crowdfunding publisher, established in 2011.

We believe that wonderful things can happen when you clear a path for people who share a passion. That's why we've built a platform that brings together readers and authors to crowdfund books they believe in – and give fresh ideas that don't fit the traditional mould the chance they deserve.

This book is in your hands because readers made it possible. Everyone who pledged their support is listed below. Join them by visiting unbound.com and supporting a book today.

Angeline B Adams
Naomi Adamson
Verity Allan
Steve Allen
Helen Anderson
Ian Andrew
Richard Ashcroft
Malcolm Balen
Mischa Balen
Rachel Balen
Robin and Elizabeth
  Balen
Carole Barnes

Julie Baskett
Stephen Baskett
Val Bayliss-Brideaux
Charlie Beaumont
Mary Beaver
Lisa Beecham
Will Bennett
The Big Anxiety
  Festival of Arts +
  Science + People
Elouise Sylvia
  Bingham
Janet Blair

Stephanie Bretherton
Adam Brignull
Catherine Brown
Darcie Burk
Leah Carden
Moira and Chris
  Cardosi
Katherine Cavill
Paul Child
Sheila Chisholm
Frances Clarke
Sally-Pomme
  Clayton

Helen & Simon Cole
Ruth Cotton
Robert Cox
Kevin Crossley-
    Holland
Heather Cueva
Sasha Curtis
Aileen Dagnall
Brian Davidson
John Davis
Poppy Davis
Rupert Davis
Jill Dawson
Lesley Dawson
Sarah de Quidt
G. Deyke
Beata Diakowska
Lynne Doggart
Joseph Elliott
Michael Elliott
Julie Erwin
Mark Farrer-Brown
Maz Finch
Ronald Forbes and
    Sheena Bell
Jo Forrester
Alexandra Forshaw
Anna Foxon
Jill Foxon
Ruth Franklin
Mairi Fraser
Peter Fremlin
Giancarlo Gemin
Patricia George-
    Zwicker
Jo Gleave
GMarkC
Katherine Gordon
Sarah Gosney-
    Davies

Christopher Grace
TheoJane Graham
Claire Greenwood
Claire and Robin
    Greenwood
Maryna Grip
Pat Haley
Sara Halter
Kate Hammer
Kate Harper
Brian and Irene
    Harrop
Pete Harrop
Pete Harrop and
    Kate Harper
Sarah Harrop and
    Les Roy
Rhian Hay
Eloise & Iris Hendry
Benjamin Hodgson
Sophie Holland
Elizabeth Houghton
Shayne Husbands
Lizzie Huxley-Jones
Rhoda Innes
Diana Jackson
Ewan Jackson
Kirsteen Jackson
Len Jemison
Sarah Ann Jemison
Emmy Maddy
    Johnston
Helen Joseph
Georgina Kamsika
Laine Kenton
Dan Kieran
Neil Kimmett
Barb Kirkham
Sam Kischkel
Majken Kruse

Paul La Planche
Ash Li
Chris Limb
Sandra Ling
Natasha Lohan
Maria Lopes
Emma Lord
Sylvia Lowery
Pauline Lygo
Bruce Macdonald
Madeline Macdonald
Andrew MacQuarrie
Iliana Magiati
Sumita Majumdar
Anika Mason
Luke Matthews
Rob Matthews
Tom Matthews
Uncle Matty
Paola McClure
Andrew McCluskey
Rebecca McCormick
Adam McDicken
Robbie Mcdicken
Carol McDonald
daniel mcdonald
Barry McKeever
Karen Meager
Ann Memmott
Caroline Miles
Amy Miller
Bryan Mitchell
John Mitchinson
Eleanor Mollett
Olivia Montoya
Alex Morrall
Nicky Muir
Dinah Murray
Carlo Navato
JG Nelson

Tom Nesbit and
    Adrienne Burke
Anna Newell
Jo Newman
Kathleen Nimmo
Sally Norris
Andrew Pankhurst
Joan Parr
Tristan Partridge
Diana Pasterfield
Esme Pears
Graham Peck
phanes
Rachel Phillips
Justin Pollard
Lucy Powrie
Jonathan Prag
Lynette and
    Richard Prag
Harriet Quint
Marcus Quint
Maxine R.
Laura Ramsey
Joe Reamer
Gideon Reed
Sara Rhoades
Duncan Ritchie
David Robertson
Ewan Roy

Ewan and Lucy Roy
Olga Ruszczak
Jonathan Ryan
Alan Salt
Damian Sawyer
Joyce Sawyer
Keith Sawyer
Nicky Sawyer
Lynda Scott
Wendy Scott
Sue Setchfield
Cherryll Sevy
Hazel Shaw
Richard Sheehan
Steve Silberman
Patrick Simpson
Faye Sinden
Kirsty Smith
Jane Sproston
Nigel Sproston
Deirdre Sullivan
Edgar Talbot
Abby Taylor
Lize Taylor
Louie Thomas
Bill Thompson
Cheyenne Thornton
Christina Toren
Jonathan Totman

Rebecca Tucker
Joe, Miff and
    Eric Tunn
Liz Tunn
Liz and Ed Tunn
Ruth Tunn
Amy Tunstall
Patricia Tyrie
Lewis Tyrrell
Margaret Vernon
Babs Viejo
Tim Wagg
Rosemary Walker
Eleanor Walsh
Abigail Walton
Andrew Weaver
Peter Wharmby
Theo Whitworth
Ann Willey
Alex Wilson
Archie Wilson
Kathryn Wilson
Lesley Wilson
Nick Wilson
Luke Winter
Nastassja Wiseman
J L Yates